COMING IN FROM THE COLD
GRAVITY #1

by Sarina Bowen

Rennie Road Books

Sarina Bowen

Copyright © 2014 Sarina Bowen, all rights reserved

Cover design: Sarina Bowen
Publication history: Published 2014 by Harlequin-e, 2015 by Rennie Road Books

Coming In From the Cold is a work of fiction. Names, places, and incidents are either products of the author's imagination or used fictitiously.

One

WILLOW NEEDED TO keep the old truck on the road and out of the snowy ditch for just one more mile.

At six o'clock on a December evening, the sky over Vermont had been dark for two hours already. She had the heater cranking on the highest setting, but still the windshield was icing over, the heavy snow plastering itself to the top of her field of vision. Willow hunched in her seat for a better view of the road. Creeping along at fifteen miles per hour, she'd be home in five minutes.

She hadn't meant to drive in blizzard conditions. She'd done her storm preparation—filling the old claw-foot bathtub with water, preparing herself for the inevitable loss of electricity. She put blocks of ice in her freezer and set the candles out on the kitchen table, with a box of matches at the ready.

She'd *almost* gotten everything right.

And then, heading into the barn to tuck the chickens in for the night, she'd opened their feed bin to find it empty. If she were snowed in for two days, as the Weather Channel predicted, she would have nothing to feed them.

"Damn it!" Willow had said, startling several of her Buff Orpington hens into a nervous flutter. Only the most stalwart remained at her feet, still hoping she would produce a pocketful of raisins.

Instead, she had turned on her heel, latching the barn door behind her. Just because Willow had never intended to become a chicken farmer didn't mean she wanted to kill off her stock. She and The Girls had a deal—clean feed for organic eggs. She meant to keep her end of the bargain.

The old truck had started right up, and she drove down her lengthy driveway and turned left, away from civilization, toward the country feed store. But snow had accumulated frighteningly fast since her outbound trip just a half hour before. Gripping the wheel, Willow saw another vehicle spotlit ahead—a green Jeep moving even more slowly than she was. Willow stepped on her brakes. But instead of stopping, she felt the sickening sensation of several tons of metal skidding to the right.

Time slowed to a crawl as the truck slid in an awkward direction toward both the Jeep and the ditch. The Jeep's taillights grew brighter as they approached, and Willow held her breath. At the last second, the Jeep seemed to leap to the left, causing Willow a moment of confusion over which of them—the Jeep or the truck—had moved so quickly. Was she still on the road?

The cab tilted abruptly to the right, and Willow felt a scream catch in her throat. But then the truck stopped suddenly, heaving her torso against the seatbelt. The force pressed a gasp from her lungs, and she bounced backward against the seat.

And then all was still.

With her heart banging away in her chest, Willow took stock. The cab listed to the right. Her wheels must have landed in the drainage culvert beside her road. At the sudden stop, Willow's feet had slipped off the pedals, and now the truck shuddered and died in place.

Immediately, the windshield began to fill with a white blanket of snow.

She took a deep breath. *You're okay. You're fine.* Thank goodness she'd been going so slowly when she lost control.

A tap on her door made Willow jump. Someone was standing outside. She grasped the window crank—the sort that dated her truck to the premodern era—and rolled down her window. A man's face—rugged, with a chiseled chin—looked back at her. He gave her an anxious frown. "Are you okay?"

"Yes?" she replied, still stunned.

"Well, now we're both stuck," he said. "I veered across the road to get out of your way, and I'm over a stump." Even in the dark she could see his handsome jaw flex with irritation.

"It's my fault that you hit a stump on the other side of the road?" Willow knew she ought to focus on the problem at hand. But the handsome stranger in front of her was every bit as distracting as their fender bender. She couldn't help but admire his sleek white jacket, of the sort of technical fabric sold at the fancy ski shops in town. He had a silver wool hat pulled down over his head, but brown curls escaped from the bottom of it, framing his eyes. He reminded her of a snow god. A slightly ornery one.

He threw up his hands. "I don't know," he huffed. "Never mind." He walked away from her. The snow was falling so fast that the blizzard swallowed him up before he'd taken five steps. He was a big man, she noticed—tall, with long legs and a tight backside.

Nice work, Willow. She had just run the most attractive guy in the county off the road.

Snow blew into her car, so Willow cranked the window closed again. Then she pressed down on the clutch and brake, turning the truck's key.

Nothing.

Damn.

Willow pumped the gas pedal a couple of times and tried the key again. And again. But the engine wouldn't even turn over.

"Oh no," Willow said aloud. "Oh no, oh no, oh no." She needed to call roadside assistance. Digging a hand into her purse for her phone, she turned it on. Willow already knew what it would say, but she looked anyway.

Searching.

She stared. "Come on."

No signal.

It was just so typical of her recent troubles. Calling for help was like so many other things in her life—an escape hatch that worked for people who weren't Willow. Other girls might have family to fall back on or catch a break financially, but she had to go and fall hard for a man so inappropriate, so uninterested in her continued happiness that he'd sealed off the exits. Her money was sunk into their old farmhouse; her credit was maxed out by his plans. And he had gone to California with another woman. There Willow sat, in a fifteen-year-old truck that wouldn't start, chicken feed in the back.

She couldn't even call 9-1-1. He'd taken that away, too. It had been *his* dream to move out to the middle of nowhere together.

And then he'd split, leaving her holding the feed bucket.

Damned Vermont. Damned snow. Damned truck. Damned cheating ex-boyfriend who'd fled to California. Damn. Damn. Damn.

* * *

Back in his Jeep, Dane Hollister smacked the steering wheel. Then he pulled the stick into reverse and tried again. But the wheels spun without catching. Whatever was holding him off the ground must be something quite large, because the Jeep had good clearance, four-wheel drive and sturdy snow tires. Only very bad luck could put him in a snowbank.

But Dane was used to being unlucky.

Calm down, he ordered himself.

He had snapped at that girl. It was true that he'd still be driving toward the town of Hamilton if she hadn't come along. But the blizzard wasn't her fault.

Dane rested his hands in his lap and analyzed the last few minutes. He'd seen the truck coming too fast. He'd turned the wheel a little too hard, and the new snow had slicked against the salted road, causing the Jeep to spin.

He probed the incident like the ski team doctor fingering tendons for an injury. But in this case, it could have happened to anyone. He had not experienced any unusual muscle reflexes. The incident was just a fluke.

It had not been caused by *a symptom*.

Dane blew out a breath, and then focused his thoughts on the real problem at hand. He was stuck about eight miles from the crappy little room he rented on Main Street. There was more than a foot of snow on the ground, and the forecast was for much more.

And he needed to apologize to the pretty girl in the ugly black truck.

He put his gloves on. Leaving the engine running, he got out. Christ. The snow was coming down fast and furious. His own headlights did little to illuminate the road, but he knew where she was—kitty-corner to him. He pointed himself in a diagonal line away from his headlights and found her. Again he knocked on her window. The cab was dark and he couldn't see inside.

"Hello?" he called.

There was no answer.

"Are you okay?" he asked again. There was only silence. Had she vanished? It was even a little creepy. But there was really only one thing in the world that Dane Hollister was afraid of, and it wasn't standing there on the road.

He grasped the handle and opened the truck's door, and there she was again. Only now there were tears drying on her face.

Nice, Dane. Good work, asshole.

The girl wiped her face quickly with her hand, embarrassed.

"Hey!" he said, in a voice that was much warmer than before. "Christ, I'm sorry. Didn't mean to flip out on you. Can I help?"

She tried to pull herself together, clearing her throat. "The truck won't start."

"Do you want me to give it a try?"

She looked up at him then, one eyebrow raised cynically. "Because I might have forgotten how to do it myself?"

He laughed. "Right. I get it. But I don't know what else to offer."

She slid across the seat, swinging her legs over the gearbox. "Go ahead. And if she starts, I won't even hold it against you."

He swung into the cab and closed the door. Then he tried to start the engine. Since the seat was set for her petite frame, his knees were jammed up against the steering column. Not that it mattered. When he turned the key, there was only silence. "She won't even turn over? Not once?"

"Not once."

He leaned back, or tried to. "Sorry. Our options for getting out of here aren't very good."

"I'll just walk it," she said. "My house is about a mile away."

"Hmm," he said quietly. He didn't want to insult her again, but unless she had a snowmobile with floodlights on it, she'd be lost before you could say *nor'easter*. "I'm not sure that's such a good idea." He groped for the high beams. "Look, the road is gone." The lights illuminated all of about four feet in front of the truck, a deep flurry of falling snow, punctuated by only blackness beyond.

"Wow," she whispered.

"Do you know any of your neighbors? I didn't see any lights…."

She shook her head, silky hair sliding over her shoulders. "There aren't many houses out here. This land is held in conservation."

"Okayyy…" he said. "I'm out of ideas. I guess we're going to have to call 9-1-1."

She tipped her head back and let out a musical laugh.

"What's so funny?"

"You're not from around here, are you?"

"Not for years," Dane admitted. He'd grown up two towns away, but that felt like a lifetime ago.

Reluctantly he turned off her headlights, saving her battery, yet plunging the cab into darkness. He'd been enjoying the sight of a pretty girl laughing, cheeks flushed, perfect pink lips smiling up at the ceiling. Just because Dane planned never to get involved with a woman didn't mean he didn't like looking at them. (Especially the occasional naked woman between his legs.) And this one was really quite extraordinary. Late twenties, slender, and with a long graceful neck. Even with the bulk of her down jacket he'd noticed a full bust that heaved as she laughed.

"There's no reception anywhere on this road," she said, "until you're almost into Hamilton."

"Right," he said. "I'd forgotten. The mobile phone companies have no love for the forty-ninth most populous state."

Dane had spent the past ten years traveling on the World Cup skiing circuit. This was his first time back in Vermont in years. Elite skiers didn't train in Vermont—the mountains weren't tall enough, and the snowfall was unreliable. Instead, they trained at the big western mountains, in Colorado or Utah.

But this year, Dane and his coach were making an exception. They'd camped here for the season—between races—to be close to Dane's latest family tragedy. In Vermont, he was able see his sick brother every week, yet keep his troubles far away from the prying eyes of the ski association.

"So…" the girl took a deep breath. "That leaves us waiting for the plow to come by. The driver can radio in for help."

Dane shifted on her uncomfortable bench seat. With the cab listing to the right, he had to hang on with the heels of his boots to avoid sliding into her. "Okay," he said. "Look, my name's Dane, and I just wanted to say that I'm sorry I barked at you before."

Her head turned in the dark. "It's okay. Skidding is scary, and it made me a little cuckoo too—I actually felt drunk for a minute there."

"Are you going to tell me your name?"

"Sorry, it's Willow Reade."

Willow. He cleared his throat. "Willow, your truck is ferociously uncomfortable. Do you mind if we wait for the plow in my Jeep? I left it running."

"Oh!" she said. "Um, sure. If that's okay. I'm kind of up against the door here."

He forced open the driver's side door. "I don't know how long we'll be waiting. Do you happen to have any emergency supplies in your glove box...whiskey? Chocolate?"

She laughed. "Sorry. I am a completely useless human."

The way she said it was bitter. As if she believed it.

Anyhow, Willow followed him toward his Jeep, which was lit by his running lights. But in every other direction it was utterly dark. "Ladies first," he said. "Do you mind climbing across? You could go around to the passenger door, but I don't know what you'd be walking into over there."

He held the door while she slid inside, climbing carefully over the automatic gearshift.

Dane closed the door behind her and walked around to the back, opening the tailgate. He saw her spin around to watch him. Quickly, so as not to let too much heat out of the car, he dragged a half dozen pairs of skis out of the back and then slammed the door. He set the skis against the back of the Jeep, in a lean-to formation.

When he opened the driver's side door again, her worried face looked up at him. He closed the door, plunging them into darkness. "I cleaned all the snow away from the tailpipe, and tented skis over it," he explained. "We should be able to run the engine for a while before the exhaust gets clogged."

"Oh!" He could hear her shiver beside him. "Thank-you, Boy Scout. It crossed my mind that you were making room for my mutilated body. But I forgot to worry about accidental asphyxiation."

"Christ," he laughed in what he hoped was a non-threatening way. "The only thing I'd like to mutilate is a cheeseburger, medium rare. And a side of onion rings."

"Good," she said. "Because it's been a pretty crappy day already."

"Has it?" He leaned back against the headrest. "Let's name all the shitty things about this day. You start."

"Well, okay," her voice was tentative. He wished he could see her face. Her tone suggested a frown across that pink, kissable mouth he'd spied earlier. "My truck may have breathed its last. And I can't afford a new one."

"I'm sorry," he said.

"Your turn," Willow pressed.

"Sure. I was supposed to drive to Keene tonight. And I have a flight out of Boston tomorrow. But the roads are trashed, and the Jeep is stuck. Your turn."

"That *is* inconvenient. I shouldn't have been on the road at all. I drove out because I needed chicken feed, which seemed important. But now I realize that I didn't check their water, and the chickens are far more likely to die of thirst than hunger. Go."

"*We* might die of thirst first. Go."

He felt her turn toward him in the dark. "I have to throw a flag on that one, mister," she said. "We're not trapped in a barn like them, we're surrounded by water. How about this: I left a pot of chili cooking in my kitchen, and it might burn. Go."

"New rule," he announced. "Let's not talk about food. I've been working out since five-thirty this morning, and lunch was five hours ago. Your turn."

"All right..." Willow sounded as if she was running out of complaints, at least the ones she was willing to tell a stranger. "There is going to be some world-class shoveling to do tomorrow."

"Well, I have to flag that one," Dane said. "Because shoveling means snow, and I live for snow. So here's the *real* bummer. We're getting two feet of freshy, and I can't ski on it tomorrow. I have to travel."

"The snow will still be here when you get back," Willow pointed out.

"You aren't a skier, are you? There's nothing like first tracks. Flying down a slope in un-tracked powder is the best thing there is. It's better than sex."

Willow burst out laughing. "You did *not* just say that."

"What?"

"I feel sorry for your girlfriend," she giggled.

"I don't have one."

But that only made her laugh harder. "Sorry, I'm no expert on skiing, so it's possible that you know something I don't. On the other hand, it's also possible that you're meeting the wrong girls."

He grinned in the dark. "Fair enough. I think it's your turn."

"Ah." She took a deep breath. "Okay, my ex called today and asked me to sell his motorcycle and wire him the money. As if that would take no effort on my part. Even though he left me in debt." Her voice quavered a bit at the end. Their little game had turned into a peculiar little confessional. "Your turn."

"My brother is dying," Dane bit out. "And I'm supposed to be driving to see him right now."

Christ. He had no idea what made him tell her that. To say that he wasn't a sharer was putting it mildly. But the dark and the warm sound of her voice had loosened up his tongue.

"I'm sorry," she whispered.

He shook his head in the darkness. "It's been a long illness. I've known it was coming."

"What's his name?" she asked.

Her choice of questions made him like her even more. It wasn't a nosy *what's wrong with him?* Instead, she'd asked something much more relevant, something which honored his brother the way Dane thought of him—a happy, laughing man. The father that Dane never had.

"He's Finn," he answered. "We're Finn and Dane. My mother had a thing for Scandinavia."

Poor Finn.

For almost fifteen years, Dane had known Finn would die. When Dane was a teenager, his brother sat him down and explained it. "It killed mom, and it will eventually kill me, too. But maybe not you, Danger man, you just keep skiing fast, and maybe you'll outrun it."

He and Finn were ten years apart. His brother had been twenty-five at the time he received his diagnosis. Poor Finn had started showing symptoms a good decade earlier than most people with the disease. Now Finn was not quite forty, and Dane was about to turn thirty.

And eventually, the symptoms would come for him, too.

No matter what his brother said, Dane was sure of it. He had spent the last fifteen years trying to accept it. And this was Dane's true secret. The fact that his brother was sick could slip out, sitting next to a silky-haired girl in a dark car…that didn't matter—not really. But nothing could shake that other truth from his lips. If anyone ever found out about the genetic time bomb that awaited him, Dane would lose his place on the ski team, his endorsements. Everything.

"It can't be easy," Willow said, her voice low. "Watching somebody die."

He lifted his arms behind his head, grabbing the headrest with both hands. "We all go someday, right?" How many times had Dane said that aloud—a million? And always with the unfortunate knowledge that while there are many ways to die, he'd seen one of the ugliest. First his mother, and now Finn.

"I guess so," she said softly.

"Including your chickens?"

She laughed. "Don't say that. They'll probably be fine. I'm just mad at myself for driving out through the storm. I've tried to become a country girl, but it just never quite stuck."

"So *you're* not from around here either, like you accused me of a little while ago…."

She laughed again, and it was a musical sound. He decided he wanted to hear that laugh a few more times before the plow truck showed up. "No, before we moved here, I lived in Manhattan for seven years. I went to NYU, and then did most of a doctorate."

"So…then you decided to move to the sticks and raise chickens?"

"Ugh. Do I have to tell this part?"

"No," he said quickly. "Not if it's painful."

"It's just painfully *stupid*," she sighed. "I followed a guy here two years ago. He was very interested in the back-to-the-land movement. Unfortunately he was also very interested in a twenty-one-year-old folk singer. So now I own a hundred-year-old farmhouse on fifteen acres, which I cannot sell. I can't get a decent job, and I can't finish my graduate degree. I'm kind of stuck, and there's nobody to blame."

"Except for the asshole."

"Except for him. But if I'd been smarter, it wouldn't have happened. Now he's in California. He's gotten smarter, too, I think. She has a trust fund."

"Christ," he said. "I'm sorry."

"Me too."

A silence fell between them. "Excuse me for a minute, I'm going to check the tailpipe," he said. He opened the door, which brought the dome light on again, and he got another look at Willow's face. This time she smiled at him, and her big hazel eyes shone. God, she was pretty. In a perfect world he could run his fingers through that hair, taste those perfect lips. Hell, if he was going to dream big, in a perfect world he could go home to something like that every night.

But not this world. Never in this one. He shut the door.

The wind whipped his face as Dane walked to the back of the car. For a moment, he couldn't see at all. The gust pushed on his chest so fiercely that he put a hand out, his fingers finding the Jeep's frame. He followed it around to the back, where his taillights revealed that snow was drifting everywhere, accumulating in spite of the wind block he'd tried to make with the skis. He kicked as much snow away from the rear of the Jeep as he could. But it was falling incredibly fast. So much for the comfort of the heater.

Two

WILLOW WAS ONLY alone for a couple of minutes, but they weren't fun ones. When he'd opened the door, the sound of the storm had been fierce. What had she done, getting stuck out here? It was just another stupid error to add to her lengthy list.

She felt much better when his door opened again, and Dane's hearty smile reappeared. With the dome light on, she could see how blue his eyes were, and the extraordinary length of his lashes. And that curly hair was delicious.

"Okay," he said, hopping back into the car and shutting the door. "Don't panic."

"Why?" Willow didn't like the sound of that.

"I've never seen accumulation like this in New England."

"Where *have* you seen it?" She made the question sound flip, to cover up her fear.

"Tahoe once. And Zermatt." He turned the heat up to full blast for a minute, rewarming the car. Then he turned the key, causing the Jeep's engine to fall silent. He flipped off the headlights, and they were plunged into complete darkness.

"What are you, a meteorologist?"

"Only during ski season," he said.

She took a deep breath. Were they going to freeze? "What *is* your day job?"

"I'm an alpine skier."

"That's a job?"

He chuckled. "It is if you don't mind going eighty miles an hour."

She swiveled her head toward him. "Seriously? You race?" No wonder he'd had numerous pairs of skis in his car, but no backseats.

"Yes, ma'am."

"Well that's fun." And, truth be told, sexy.

"It is, except when it isn't."

"And when is that?"

"When I lose. Or crash. Usually those things happen at the same time."

She laughed. "What, you never just lose?"

"I'm famous for blowing up. Go big or go home, as the saying goes."

"Wait…Dane. What's your last name?"

"Hollister."

"No way! Danger Hollister. That's you? The…Olympian?"

"It is. Silly name and all."

"Did your mother really name you Danger?"

"No. I changed it to Danger from plain old Dane when I joined the circuit."

"Why?" she laughed.

"Because I was twenty-one…seemed like a good idea at the time."

"What does it say on your driver's license?"

He fumbled in the dark for something in a pocket. Then he pressed the dome light with his hand and leaned toward her. "Feast your eyes on this."

She belly laughed. DANGER HOLLISTER was spelled out. She looked up at him, and his blue eyes flashed with humor. Willow relaxed a little then. She was stuck in a Jeep with no heat, in a blizzard. But sitting next to him, it was almost fun.

He shut the light off again. "That plow is taking its sweet time."

"They usually do a pretty good job on this road," she said. "The ski hill is the only reason why. The rich people have to be able to get to their vacation condos." Then she realized her mistake. "I'll take my foot out of my mouth now."

"Nah, I think you called it pretty well," he said. "But those rich people keep me in business. Ski races don't bring in money for the little mountains. But we need the little mountains to keep the sport alive."

"What are you doing here in Hamilton?" she asked him.

"Training solo for a while," he said, "between races. It puts me here on and off until spring."

Willow rubbed her hands on her arms. With the car's engine off, it was getting cold. She reached for the hood of her jacket, but it wasn't to be found. Willow had unzipped it last week and left it in the mudroom of her house. "Of course."

"What's that?"

"Nothing," she sighed. "Just marveling at my own stupidity again. I do that on the half hour."

"Are you cold?" he asked. "Wait..." He reached around between their seats. "Can't reach it..." He swiveled his big frame to lean back between the seats, finally emerging with something bulky. She heard a plastic click, and then a wad of what felt like a comforter unfolded between them.

"You keep a sleeping bag in your car?" she asked.

"For emergencies," he said. "I drive around in a lot of bad weather. But usually I pull it out for crashing on other people's hotel-room floors." She heard the sound of a zipper. "Here," he said. "Hold this corner."

She met his hands in the dark and took the corner of the comforter. He pulled the zipper all the way around. "There," he said, pushing his end under the steering wheel. Then he reached below his chair to slide the driver's seat backward. "We might as well wait in comfort."

"True. And thank-you, by the way. I'd be shivering in my truck right now."

"Don't mention it," he said.

Her heart beat rapidly, and she didn't even know why. There was something intimate about sitting there with him under the sleeping bag. After only an hour in his company, she had a crush on him. She reached for the bar under her seat and slid herself back a bit, too. "Now if only we had a movie and some popcorn," she said. "It would be like any other night at my house."

"You mentioned food again," he complained. "Cut it out, woman."

"I do make good popcorn. The trick is coconut oil and just the right amount of salt."

"You are killing me right now." His laugh warmed her almost as well as the sleeping bag.

* * *

They fell silent for a little while. Dane listened to the sound of Willow's breathing, only a few feet away. He tried on the image of watching a movie at home—a quiet night with a girl like her. It wasn't very often that he allowed himself to think like this, to marvel at the strangeness of his life. Half the men in New England were probably, at this very moment, snuggled up on sofas next to women, watching a movie on TV. That's what people did during blizzards.

People who were not Dane.

Relationships of any kind were off the table for him. So he never snuggled up to anyone, never tucked his feet onto a coffee table alongside a woman's, never rolled over in bed to find another warm body there.

He wasn't a monk, of course. Fucking was different. He did plenty of that. But because he maintained a strict policy—one-night stands only—he'd never *slept* with anyone in the literal sense, never fallen asleep next to a lover. Not since he was a teenager, anyway. After he'd truly understood that his life would never have a happy ending, he never had a girlfriend. He would never be married. No woman would say "I do" to that—to watching him deteriorate, to wiping the drool off his face.

On the racing circuit there was always a female skier—or fan—willing to open her legs for him. Dane always stated his terms clearly ahead of time. And even then, he'd rarely been refused, especially since he'd begun winning World Cup events. Gold medals were a potent aphrodisiac. There was one skier in particular—Kelli— with whom he'd shared multiple one-night stands. And yes, there was such a thing. A few times a season, when the pressure of the tour got to him, he'd request a second hotel room key card from the front desk. A Swede, Kelli knew only slightly more English than he knew Swedish—which was almost none. When he offered her the card, wordlessly of course, she always took it.

Late in the night—which was around eleven for an elite skier, since their days began early—she would enter his room silently and shed all her clothes. They would suck and nibble and slam each other for an hour or two. And when they were sated, she always disappeared again without a word.

She was perfect for him.

But now here he was, sporting a hard-on in the seat of his frigid Jeep. And all because he was sitting beneath a sleeping bag—with a very pretty girl, but still—like any dope. The racing life was plenty exciting, but tonight it didn't feel like enough. At that moment, he wanted what dudes with beer guts and bald heads had. He wanted the pretty girl to lay her head on his shoulder and ask him to please change the channel or to bring her a drink.

He shucked off his gloves and rubbed his face with his hands.

"What's the matter?"

I'm stupid, too, he wanted to say. "My blood sugar is crashing," he said instead. "If we're lucky, you might find a couple of energy bars in the glove box."

He heard her opening it, then fumbling around inside. "Score," she said. He heard the crinkle of plastic. "Here."

Dane held out his hands in the dark. She found him, and a gloved hand fumbled two bars into his palm. He dropped the bars into his lap, and then caught her hand before it moved away. "Hang on," he said, pulling her glove off, then clasping her hand in both of his. Her skin was soft, and it was difficult to let her go. "Okay," he said. "You're not too bad off." He put her glove back into her hand.

* * *

A tingle went up the back of Willow's neck as two giant hands released hers. "What was that for?" she asked, voice husky.

"If your hands aren't cold, then your core is warm enough," he said, his voice low.

"Oh," she whispered.

"It's basic cold-weather safety. Do you want peanut butter or oatmeal raisin?" he asked.

Her cheeks flushed, and she was glad for the dark. "You go ahead and enjoy them," she said.

"No way. I insist on sharing this feast."

"What a gentleman," she remarked, smiling. "Surprise me."

"Good choice, because I can't read the labels." He cracked one package open. "Hold out your hands."

She did, and his found them again. She tried not to be overly conscious of his touch in the dark as he put an energy bar carefully into her palm. "Thanks."

He didn't answer. She only heard him open his and chew.

They ate in silence, and Willow tried to stomp out her unlikely attraction to this stranger. But something in his delivery really spoke to her. His smoky voice in the dark hinted at secrets. She wished he would reach for her hands again, and this time forget to let go.

"So," he said after a time. "How was he an asshole?"

"Oh, my boyfriend? He..." *He never loved me.* "I fell hard, and he didn't. And I lived that way for two years, hoping things would get better. But he only wanted a fan club. And a house to live in."

"That's rough," Dane said, his voice a pleasing rumble. Silence descended on them for a moment. And then he said, "Do you hear something?"

She strained to listen. And between gusts of wind she did hear something—an engine.

Dane turned the key in the ignition, and the car hummed to life. He put on the hazard lights, the headlights and the windshield wipers. As Willow watched, a thick blanket of snow was swished off of the glass in front of her. "Wow," she said as the headlights slowly became visible. "You weren't kidding about the accumulation."

Dane whipped around in his seat, trying to see out the back, where another wiper had cleared off the rectangular rear window. "It's back there," he said.

"Yay," Willow said, but she was a liar. As ridiculous as it sounded, she wasn't quite ready for their peculiar tryst to end. Her darkened farmhouse was drafty and lonely.

"We need more light," Dane said, hitting the dome light over his head. "Getting *hit* by the plow would not be the best way to finish this evening."

She spun around to watch, too, and their heads were nearly touching. The glow of headlamps grew faintly visible. Though it still had to be a hundred yards away, Willow thought she could make out the yellow-orange flasher that sat atop municipal vehicles. "He'll definitely stop for us, won't he?" she worried.

"Sure, unless he's a total dick. Like your ex-boyfriend." Gently, he knocked his knit hat into her knit hat, just once. Like a special wintertime fist bump.

She laughed, her eyes fixed on the plow truck. When this was over, she was going to ask for his phone number. He was quite a guy, Danger Hollister.

Three

As the light grew brighter, Dane knew he was supposed to feel relieved. But all it meant for him was safe passage to another lonely night in his room over on Main Street, keeping company with a copy of *Sports Illustrated* and some tunes. Or worrying about Finn, the last person alive who really knew him.

Then, as Dane watched, the plow truck turned the corner, heading onto another road. "What the...?"

The dome light was still on, and he turned to Willow, who did not look surprised. "I thought that could happen," she said.

"Why?"

"We're very close to the town line. We're sitting in Westland, and I'll bet the plow belongs to Hamilton. And he must not have seen us here."

"Or maybe the driver *was* your ex?"

Those beautiful lips curved into a smile, and she punched him in the arm. "This one's not on me. Maybe it was one of yours."

"Right," he said, his eyes stuck on her feminine smile. He pressed the dome light off again, reluctantly.

Jokes aside, one benefit of being a loner was that he didn't actually have any ex-girlfriends. The other guys on the circuit had plenty of trouble with those. He turned off the headlights, and turned the key in the ignition. The car fell silent.

"What do we do now?" Willow asked. He was pleased to hear that her tone was playful, not scared.

"Oh, I think we have a beer," he said.

"It would be really nice if you weren't kidding."

Dane felt around the lower part of the driver's side door. His hands closed around the bottle. He took the keys from the ignition and fumbled with the church key he kept there, popping the top. "You can have the first sip. Give me your hands. We can't spill a drop."

"*Seriously*? You have a beer?"

He found her fingers, and curled them around the bottle. "Give you a dollar if you can tell me the brand."

Laughing, she took a sip. "Saint Pauli Girl."

"No fucking way!"

She giggled. "You left the hazards on, and I know the label. The girl in the German costume, with the big tatas…."

He hit the button to shut off the hazards. "Cheater."

"I can't believe you just happened to have a beer in your car."

"The ski tech gave me a roadie. I forgot about it until the energy bar made me thirsty."

"Here," she said, passing it back to him. He managed to put his hands on hers while taking the bottle, and again while passing it back to her after a swig. What was up with that? He hadn't been so eager to touch anyone's hand since about the eighth grade.

"You don't secretly have a six pack, I suppose?" she asked.

"No," he smiled. "I wish I did. But then we'd have to pee."

The joke caught her while sipping, and she choked a little.

"Easy," he said. "That's precious liquid you're holding."

She passed it back. "I didn't spill. I swear." With the lights off again, it was very, very dark. He couldn't see her at all, and the effect seemed to sharpen his awareness of her sounds in the dark. Each exhalation, each word she spoke, sounded intimate.

"A full bladder is only useful if you're trapped in an avalanche, not in a Jeep," he said, keeping the banter alive.

"Why is a full...? Never mind. I don't want to know."

"Wise girl." He took a tiny sip and passed the bottle back, executing a full-contact hand-off.

They sipped slowly to make the bottle last, but it went fast anyway. "You finish it," he said, turning in his seat to face her.

"Okay," she said, downing the last sip. "But only because I have one more thing to add to this party."

This time, when she handed the bottle back, he caught her hand and did not let go. "What's that?" he asked, wondering how she would react. Her fingers were slim and delicate.

She paused before answering, and he wondered if he'd overstepped. But she didn't pull her hand away. "My pocket is full of raisins," she said eventually.

"Your pocket?" She still didn't pull away. So he put his other hand on top of hers.

"Yeah," she breathed. "They were supposed to be a treat for my chickens. But I promise there's no chicken spit on them or anything."

He pressed her small hand flat between his two, rubbing her knuckles gently. "Do chickens have spit?" he asked.

"No," she whispered.

Hopefully he wasn't the only one who found their grade school touch exciting. "I didn't know that," he said. He turned her hand over in his, stroking it.

* * *

What the hell was happening here? Willow had never thought of her palm as a sexual organ before, but the sensation of his fingertips on her skin was electric. "Do you like raisins?" she asked, stupidly.

"Sure," he said.

Willow put her free hand into her pocket. "So, how about you tell me something... I know—something that you've learned from life experience. And I'll give you one."

He chuckled, dragging his thumb slowly down her palm. "Something I've learned the hard way. How about this: gravity never takes a day off. You learn that pretty quick in my line of work."

"Hmm," Willow said, distracted by his touch. "That's a bit obvious, but I'll give it to you." She pulled a raisin out of her pocket, passing it into one of his hands.

He briefly let go of her to pop it into his mouth. "Thank-you," he said, finding her hand again in the dark. "Now you tell me something wise."

"All right," she said. "I never planned to raise chickens, but watching them has been fascinating. You can take three-day-old chicks, who have never seen a hen, and never been out of a cardboard box, and they'll peck at the cornmeal you feed them. But if you put a worm in there, they go nuts, fighting over it. They're crazy for worms, even though they've never seen one before. Instinct is real."

And wasn't that the truth. Because she was feeling a whole lot of instinct, all of a sudden.

"Well, that is cool," Dane said. He was still massaging her hand, his thumb warming her palm. "If I get to judge, I'd say you win a raisin."

Willow popped one into her mouth. "Your turn."

"Okay," Dane said, "I've learned that airplane food is universally bad, no matter where you go in the world. That's not just a cliché."

This time, when Willow brought a raisin toward him in the dark, he caught her hand and raised it to his mouth. Her palm brushed his chin as he guided the raisin to his lips. "Thanks," he whispered. "So it's your turn."

She laced her fingers in his. His hand was so much bigger than hers. So warm and strong. "Hmm…I've learned that you can keep guacamole from turning brown by pressing plastic wrap across the surface."

"There you go again, mentioning food," he scolded.

His fingers brushed the sensitive skin above her wrist, and Willow was glad that the darkness prevented him from seeing her face. The sensation made her close her eyes. "But *you* mentioned food," she whispered. She was beginning to feel giddy. Being trapped in a car in a storm should have made her feel stupid. Instead, she was pointlessly and inappropriately happy.

"*Big* difference. I mentioned *bad* food. Your homemade guacamole versus airplane food—in a cage match, who wins?"

"My guacamole, of course," she giggled. "But you have no way of knowing that. Come on. Tell me something empirically true, and I'll give you another raisin."

He sighed, and the sound of it made her wish she could feel his breath against her face. "Okay. If you don't look at the needle, it really does hurt less."

Well, *that* was a bit dark. "Sure…" Her pulse began to race. It was crazy to touch this stranger. It was crazy, and she really wasn't the type. But something about him made it difficult to stop. Willow reached into her pocket and retrieved another raisin. This time, she raised it to his mouth herself, sweeping her finger very deliberately across his lower lip before slipping it onto his tongue. He closed his lips, catching her two fingers in his mouth. He sucked the tip of her forefinger as she pulled it away.

Good God, it was sexy.

"Your turn," he whispered.

Willow felt light-headed. That was the only explanation she could give for what she said next. "Lately," she whispered, "I've learned that not all bad days end that way." It was too dark to read his expression, even if she were brave enough to look.

In answer, he squeezed her hand. Then he tugged gently on it, pulling her toward himself. Willow held her breath, wondering if he was about to do what she hoped he was about to do.

It was very, very dark.

She felt his breath on her face before his lips found her cheekbone. He paused there, for two beats of her heart, his mouth offering a sensuous brush against her skin. Then, with a sigh, he turned his chin to find her mouth. The first kiss was small, a sweep of soft lips across hers, coming to rest at the sensitive corner of her mouth. "Is this okay?" he whispered. The words vibrated on her face. "If you tell me to fuck off, I'll understand."

Willow answered him by brushing the tip of her nose very gently up the length of his face and then down again. Dane's next kiss brought his soft mouth over hers. And again he paused. But it was less a hesitation than a moment of heightened anticipation. Her heart practically stopped beating while she waited for his next move. And then his lips parted her own, his tongue sliding inside. And when she met him there, tasting him, he gave a low moan, and the sound made her heart skitter.

She felt both of his hands rise to the nape of her neck, his fingers detouring under her knit hat, into her hair. Then she was pulled closer, his kisses drinking her in, nibbling her lips, scorching her tongue. The effect was exhilarating, and suddenly her body was too far from his, the damned car too constraining. She wanted to feel her own arms encircling him, to know more about him than quick glimpses had allowed. But Willow had to content herself with a half-decent grip on his shoulders, which felt powerful under her hands.

Her conscience gave her a half-hearted poke. *Willow, you are making out with a stranger in his Jeep.*

No, she told herself. She was making out with a sexy snow god during a blizzard. And yes, she was sure there was a difference.

Around them, the night was utterly silent. The wind had died. Willow cocooned against him, under their makeshift blanket, while the Jeep became covered with snow. The whole world fell away, except for the slide of his lips on hers, the strokes of his tongue against her own, and the sweep of his hands through her hair.

"Willow," he breathed when they eventually came up for air. "I love your name."

"Mmm," she said, enjoying the tickle of his hair against her forehead. "I'm not sure what they were thinking when they gave it to me."

He gave her a tiny kiss. "You never asked?"

"Never got the chance," she breathed. "I haven't seen my parents since I was four." But that was a potential mood killer right there, so she raised her hands to his face, sweeping her thumbs gently across his cheekbones, and then down onto his lips, until he shivered.

"Possibly," he said, kissing her again. "They were thinking, willows bend, but they don't break."

She smiled in the darkness. "You know, I've heard that one before."

He kissed her, laughing. They could just not keep their mouths off of each other. "You aren't afraid to call me on my bullshit. Most people don't do that."

"They don't?" In spite of the cold night, Willow felt hot all over. "They should."

He kissed her again, and she felt it everywhere. "Willow," he breathed. "I would move this party to the back of my Jeep," he said, "but that might be a bad idea."

"Why?" she panted, hating the sound desperation in her question.

"I'm not boyfriend material," he said. "I'm just passing through, and I wouldn't want you to do anything you'd regret."

He kissed her again, his mouth trailing from her lips to under her ear, to her throat, which made her head spin. She reached both hands under his cap, knitting her fingers into his curls.

His hands found the zipper of her jacket, drawing it partway down. But then he stopped. "I don't mean to be blunt," he whispered. "But it would be a one-night-only offer."

Ouch. "How pragmatic of you. Settling for me," she said.

"What?" he pulled away, his voice cautious.

"Since you can't ski the fresh powder, you might as well go with the sex." She put her fingers on his lips so she could feel him smile.

"Christ," he laughed. "I really shouldn't have said that," he said, kissing her fingers, then taking them into his mouth.

"Here's a tip," Willow said. "If you ever decide to be somebody's boyfriend, don't mention your preference."

He leaned in, his lips finding her neck in the dark. "And in the meantime?" he half kissed, half spoke. His tongue on her collarbone sent a shiver of longing down into her core.

Willow was finding it hard to think. So far, her biggest mistakes in life had been made by giving her heart away for keeps. Her last relationship had been a disaster because she had expected way too much. Dane's offer was, at least, very honest. And she wanted him. It was crazy, but she did.

"In the meantime," she whispered, shocked at herself already, "we steam up your Jeep."

He chuckled, pushing the coat off her shoulders. Then he kissed her again, his mouth smoldering hers with more heat and longing than she had felt in a good long time. By the time she found the zipper on his jacket, nobody was laughing.

Willow tried one more time to conjure some sort of remorse over her actions, but found she could not. A long tangle of life's events had conspired to lead her here, to this very moment. She didn't know why that was. She only knew she didn't want to run away.

Breaking off their kiss, Dane gathered the sleeping bag off their laps and tossed it into the back. She heard a rustle while he kicked off his boots, and then pulled his seat as far forward as he could. "You go first," he said.

With a shaky breath, Willow scooted between the seats and into the back.

She was straightening out a corner of the sleeping bag when he very awkwardly climbed back to join her. "Where'd you go?" he whispered. "Having second thoughts?"

"Not exactly," she said. "I just can't believe where the night ended up, that's all."

"No pressure," he said.

She slid nearer to him and stole his knit cap. This she tossed into the front seat, and then she scooped her hands into his hair. He wrapped her into a kiss, lifting the hem of her sweater. The sweep of his hands across her bare back combined with his tongue in his mouth was an exhilarating combination. He worked his thumbs up her torso, skimming her bra. "I want these clothes gone," he said, his voice husky. "I swear I won't let you freeze."

"You first," she whispered. Willow gripped his T-shirt in her hands and raised it over his head. Once he shrugged it off, her hands explored his chest. God, he was hard as nails under her hands. Athletes, *wow*. She skimmed his pecs, ducking her head to lick his nipples, which were hardened by the chill. Her hands ventured down his stomach, coming to rest on his belt buckle.

He interrupted her to tug her sweater upward.

"I said '*You first,*'" she whispered, grasping his fly.

"*Okayyy*," he said. He was probably used to being in charge. But the situation was too raw, too far outside her comfort zone to abandon all control. He cooperated, stilling himself while she worked to unzip his jeans.

When she'd managed the task, he pressed his hands down on the floor and lifted his hips, giving her free reign to tug his pants off him. She took his jeans and his briefs together, pulling them down around his thighs.

"Hell, it really *is* cold," he chuckled.

She worked his jeans off of him entirely. "I'll let you keep your socks, under the circumstances," she said. As she said this, she let her hands begin to trace a path back up his legs, sweeping his shins, his knees.

She took her time exploring his massive quads. He was solid muscle, as if carved from wood. She pressed his thighs apart with her hands and was rewarded with a hum of expectation. Gingerly, she moved one hand further back and onto his balls, which she stroked lightly, earning a moan. Then, still not rewarding him with the touch he really wanted, she climbed onto his legs, wrapping hers around behind him. Only then did she reach down between their bodies and slip her hand around his cock. He gasped, and she nearly did, too. Because Dane was a very big boy.

"Cold now?" she whispered.

He didn't answer. Instead he wrapped her in powerful arms and kissed her like a starving man, crushing her lips to his. As his tongue plundered her mouth, she stroked his shaft. When he groaned, she straddled him even more tightly, hugging him with her legs. The feel of his cock through the fabric of her jeans was tantalizing.

A one-night-only offer. His words echoed through her head. But what a night it was turning out to be. Dane's touch was worshipful. Each time she shivered with

35

pleasure, he kissed her. And when she touched him—her hands skimming his back, he sighed from deep in his chest. He was a puzzle—confident with his hands and his kisses, yet seemingly starving for affection.

This time, when he lifted her sweater over her head, she did not protest.

Four

DANE TOOK A deep breath as he tossed her sweater aside. *Don't rush,* he ordered himself. Usually he fucked like he skied—leaning in hard, diving for the finish line. But this girl was something different—soft curves and warm hands. Her touch lingered, and it made him want her hands on his body for as long as possible.

He wished he could see her better, but the silent darkness held its own pleasures. As the snow continued to bury the Jeep, there were no sounds except for the sighs she made as his tongue stroked hers. Willow was turning out to be surprisingly adventurous. Yet at the same time, she was no pushover. He couldn't imagine a sexier combination.

He let his palms slide down her small shoulders and slim arms. His two hands could nearly reach around her waist. When he skimmed back up, fingering the silk of her bra, her breath hitched. And the sound of her, and that her two hands were gently stroking his dick, took him back to his days as a horny teenager. He was practically ready to burst.

Gently, he pushed her hands off of his cock. "Lie down for me." Cupping her head in one hand, he tipped her onto her back. She adjusted herself so that her head lay in one corner of their little makeshift room, allowing her to stretch out. Diagonally, and with her knees bent, she just fit.

Kneeling over her, he skimmed a hand over her jeans and up past her bare stomach. His fingers paused on her sternum, where he could feel her heart beating madly beneath his hand. Dane leaned down, putting his lips onto her chest. He opened his mouth, his tongue caressing her skin. His fingers went to the cups of her silk bra, the nipples straining under his touch.

She surprised him then, gripping his head in her hands, turning his chin slightly and resting his ear on her chest. With both arms, she held him there, smoothing his hair away from his forehead, cradling him. He closed his eyes and listened to the sound of her body circulating her blood, the muscle beating away beneath the surface. He was pinned to it—her heart—the one part of a girl he had always vowed never to touch.

Weirdly, he felt an unfamiliar prickle behind his eyes.

Beneath him, Willow took a deep, steadying breath. Maybe she felt it, too. There was something happening here that was startling in its intensity. She held him there for a moment, her fingers curled into his hair, and then finally released his head. He reared up, only to bring his face down again between her breasts. He pushed her bra aside with his chin, his tongue landing on her nipple.

She whimpered, and the sound went straight to his cock. The darkness denied him the ability to see her. Yet each tiny sound she made, each little breathy exhalation told him everything he needed to know. He fumbled under her back, releasing her bra. He drew it away, then cupped both of her breasts in his hands. As he flicked his tongue across her nipples, she began to shiver, her hips shifting with obvious desire.

Dane nosed down toward her belly button, his fingers making quick work of the fly on her pants. He worked her jeans down over her hips. Then he kissed a line over the strap of her bikini underwear. When he skimmed his lips over the triangle of silk that covered her, Willow moaned.

He left one teasing hand there, rising up to lean over her mouth with a kiss. His wet lips skimmed hers, his tongue seeking her out. "Willow," he rasped. "I have a condom in my jacket. Should I get it out?"

She wrapped her arms around his neck. "Yes."

He pulled both of them into a sitting position, then he reached into the front seat.

Whoever first called it "getting lucky" was a smart man. As Dane fumbled into his jacket pocket, he had never felt so lucky.

When he ripped the packet open, and she tried to take it from him. "I've got it," he said. If you want something done right, you have to do it yourself. He wasn't a careful man on the ski hill, but he was careful about this. Every time. After he rolled the condom on, he reached for Willow, pulling her across his lap. "You still have too many clothes on," he said.

She didn't argue the point.

He slid his thumb inside her panties, then pushed them down. When they fell away, he slipped his fingers down her belly, into the sweet petals of her sex. Christ, she was wet and perfect. He felt her breath hitch as his fingers began to circle and tease. He'd planned to spend the night alone, the way he spent all of them. Instead, there was a beautiful girl writhing in his arms, her hair falling against his bare chest.

Even in his ugly life, there were moments of perfection.

"Tell me what you like," he whispered, his fingertips slicking her opening. And her answer made his cock throb.

"I just want you inside me."

She sat up a little then, turning to straddle him, her knees on the floor. When she grasped the base of his cock, he held his breath. And then it was happening. Inch by slow inch, the tight heat of her body enveloped him. "God, you feel good," he panted. "Take me deep."

Willow had to widen her legs to take him all the way in, and when her bottom came to rest against his thighs, he couldn't help but groan. They were nose to nose, and she held her body still for several long beats of his heart. The anticipation was killing him. He longed to flip her onto her back and drill into her. Somehow, he found enough patience to merely nip her lower lip with his teeth instead.

"Is this what you want?" she whispered. Slowly, she pressed upward, her hips grazing his abs. When she sank onto him again, at the same dragging pace, an impatient gasp escaped his own lips. He curved his hands around her hips, and then he lifted her, using his quads for leverage. He steered her up again, along his shaft, fucking her even though she was straddling him.

After several strokes, she was panting, too.

"Wrap your legs around me," he said.

Willow did, and was eased onto her back.

He braced his two feet against different panels of the Jeep, and thrust. "Oh," she moaned beneath him. He slicked his tongue over her lips, and she moaned again. Her hips rolled beneath him with wordless encouragement. He found a rhythm, his cock and his tongue working together.

"Don't ever...stop," she gasped.

He smiled against her lips. Everything about her was sweet—the way she moaned into his mouth, the tickle of her hair against his face. He closed his eyes and sank into the feel of her, slick and tight around him. Her breathing became shallow, little whimpers escaping her lips when he thrust.

The sound of her pleasure curled into an empty place in his chest he'd never known was there. She was perfect— soft everywhere he was hard. He was so turned on that he wouldn't last much longer. And because he was all too aware of the cruel way that life's best moments ended too quickly, he missed her already.

"So good," she whispered, her breath coming in erotic gasps.

"Give it to me," he whispered. "Come, you sweet thing." He ground his hips against hers.

Her moan started low, from her belly. And then her breasts heaved, and she cried out. The sound sent a charge right through him. He wanted to remember that sound—to store it in his heart, saving it for the solitary hours he was sure to face later. He let go then, chasing down his own climax as she gasped beneath him. He pumped into her again and again before finally stilling himself inside her.

She lay panting in his arms, one hand over her eyes. He pushed it away, and kissed her on the eyebrow.

"God," she gasped. "Wow."

"Wow," he agreed. He kissed her again, his lips still seeking a connection though his body was spent. He pulled out reluctantly, tying off the condom. It went into a cup holder. There would be something to remember to throw out tomorrow, and certainly before he had a passenger in his car. Christ.

Then he folded himself into the space next to Willow, gathering her up in his arms. He wasn't done touching her yet. He wanted more of the feel of her skin under his hands, the curve of her breast in his palm, the fresh smell of her hair. "You're quiet," he said.

"Mmm," she said, curling tighter to him. "Is that so wrong?"

"No." *Fool.* What did he want, anyway? An award? But there was something about this girl that was different. For some reason, he cared what she thought.

Willow reached behind herself and curled the edge of the sleeping bag over her back.

"Cold?" he asked.

She ran a finger down his nose. "I wasn't before. But I am now."

"Well…" he thought about it. "There's really only one way this works." He sat up, feeling around the edges of the sleeping bag. When he found the zipper's beginning, he hooked it together, and began to zip. "Roll this way, sweet thing," he said, tapping her on the knee. A minute later, he'd zipped her up.

She put a hand on his bare knee. "What about you?"

"I'll get dressed."

She sat up. "No, come here." She unzipped the bag halfway. "You first."

"We won't fit."

"I know a way." She moved aside, gathering some things from the front seat.

He slid into the bag, lying on his side.

"Put your head on this," she said, handing over his jacket. After a bit of rustling and flapping about, he felt her feet slide into the bag with his. She'd put her sweater on, and so her bare bottom tucked up against him, but her top was outside the bag, covered by her clothes.

He cupped her hip in his hand and pulled her close. She settled her head onto her own jacket and tucked herself further into the bag, curving her upper body out of the half-unzipped side to make room for his shoulders. He put an arm around her waist and curled even more tightly around her. "I like your way," he whispered.

"My way rocks," she said. Then she cleared her throat. "If I ask you a question, will you promise not to laugh?"

Uh oh, he thought. Here it comes—the moment he would have to let her down. "What?"

"Do you think…are we in danger out here, if the plow doesn't show up until morning?"

He kissed her ear, relieved. "No. The people who die in blizzards are the ones who leave their cars. Besides—it's only thirty degrees tonight. At minus twenty, we'd be worried." Then he thought of something, which made him laugh.

"You said you wouldn't laugh at my question," Willow complained.

"I'm not. I was just thinking about the protocol for surviving subzero temps." He stroked her hip. "It looks a lot like *this*." He gave her a squeeze to emphasize how close they were.

He felt Willow's giggle through her body before he heard it. "I knew that," she said. "That's why I agreed to climb back here."

"That was your reason, huh?" he teased, stroking her breast.

"Mmm-hmm," she said, snuggling against him.

A while later, her breathing evened out and she drifted off. But Dane did not. Even though he'd been up since the ass crack of dawn, he did not feel drowsy. His skin tingled with surprise at his proximity to her. And he drank it in. Because it would never happen again.

It was so quiet. There was more light now, he noticed. The Jeep's back window had avalanched. And the moon had risen, its beams filtered through a wicked thick layer of clouds. He lay there listening a long time, and eventually the growl of a motor approached. Several minutes later the yellow lights of the plow truck went by. And Dane did not even consider flagging it down.

Five

"WILLOW," A VOICE whispered.

She opened her eyes. "Ohhh," she groaned, her shoulder stiff. The surface beneath her was hard as nails.

"It's almost dawn, sweet thing," a voice said. "And the plow truck went by."

She rolled onto her back, toward the warmth. "It did?" She began to wake up, startled to see a pair of blue eyes looking down into hers.

"Twice," Dane said. "So the snow won't be up to our knees when we walk out of here."

"Okay," she said, sitting up. Her leg brushed against Dane's obvious erection. She felt her face get hot at the memory of last night.

He skimmed a hand along her hip. "I'm sorry to wake you."

"Had to be done," she said. "Did you look outside?" She could see only out of the back window of the Jeep. Everywhere she looked out there, it was white.

He turned to look. "Powder day." His fingers caressed the base of her neck, and she closed her eyes.

She had to clear her head.

"Is it time to call a tow truck from my house?" she offered. "I keep an old rotary at home for when the power goes out."

"I will take you up on that," he said.

"How about breakfast while we wait for the tow truck?"

"Mmm," he said, kissing her hair. "Now we're talking."

* * *

After the awkward trick of redressing in the Jeep—her panties eluded her until she found them under the driver's seat—they crawled out.

"Looks like we got a good foot and a half," Willow said. But it was hard to tell, as the snow had drifted everywhere.

"Anything you need from your truck?" he asked, tossing his skis back into the Jeep.

She stared at the snow-covered mound that was her truck. "No. Except for chicken feed. But it's not portable."

"No? Why."

"I buy fifty-pound bags. The Girls can wait one more day. They won't starve."

But Dane pulled on his gloves and went over to her truck. He lowered the tailgate. Then he brushed a ridiculous amount of snow off the back and hefted a bag of chicken feed off the stack.

"You know my house is about a mile away, right?"

"You know I squat four-hundred pounds at the gym every morning, right?"

She shook her head. "Better you than me."

"Let's walk, then," he said.

* * *

With the road cleared, it was easy going underfoot. Willow found herself tongue-tied. The strapping stranger at her side would be gone in an hour or two, and she didn't know what to think about that. They walked in silence while Willow planned the breakfast she would make for him. Her stove ran on propane, and even if the power was out, she could still light it.

"Willow, are you a coffee drinker?" Dane asked.

"Hell, yes. And I can manage some form of coffee whether or not I have power. Coffee is non-negotiable."

He hitched the feed bag further up onto his shoulder. "I knew I liked you."

The words gave her heart a little squeeze. She wanted that—for him to like her. She wanted to ask him a hundred questions about his life, to get to know him, to stare into those blue eyes. But he'd been very clear that their friendship was not meant to develop. Was that really true, or had he only meant to keep his options open?

She was not going to bring it up. "That's my mailbox up ahead," she said, pointing. "See?"

"I've passed that place," he said. "There's a *For Rent* sign outside. Going somewhere?"

"I wish," she said. "I would sell, but I'm underwater on the mortgage. That sign, though, is just for a furnished one-bedroom apartment I have in back of the house. The previous owner had his mother-in-law living there."

"Huh," Dane said. "Your sign should *say* it's for a one-bedroom apartment, no? I passed it by many times, thinking there was no way I'd rent a whole house. And I ended up in a seedy room over on Main Street. Fix your sign, and you'll rent it to some ski tech on the mountain within the week."

There was a silence, while Willow mourned the loss of Dane, and his powerful quadriceps, living on her property. Then she laughed. "I'll fix it today. The lack of rent money has kept me up nights all month."

"I didn't mean to harsh on your sign," Dane said.

"It's okay. I'm kind of a fuckup," Willow said.

"I doubt that," Dane argued.

You really have no idea, she said to herself. Aloud, she continued, "We're here, except for the climb."

"Nice," he said, looking up the long driveway at the house.

Willow followed his gaze to the white gables and the peaked roof. It did look nice. But for her it was a trap, a financial mistake that was standing between her and her dreams.

When they reached the side door, and she put her hand on the knob.

"Where does this go?" he asked, pointing at the bag on his shoulder.

"Just set it down, and I'll move it later," she said. "You've done the heavy lifting, as they say."

He jutted his chin toward the barn. "Over there? It's no trouble."

She hesitated for only a second. "Well, thank-you, sir. Let me get the barn door." She ran ahead to open it. The wind had blown much of the snow out of her path—it was only a foot deep most places. But Willow had to quickly shovel a snowdrift away from the entrance. When she opened it, the chickens came running toward the light. "Hi, girls!" she called. They gathered around her ankles, pecking at her jeans. She waded into the fray, grabbed the empty feed bin and pulled off the top. "Just drop it right in here," she said. "I'll deal with the bag later."

He let it fall into the bin, and the chickens scattered from the sound. They ran away clucking, feathers flying.

Dane laughed. "They're so…chicken," he said.

"It's really true," Willow agreed. "They're afraid of everything. I have a red raincoat, and if I wear it into the barn they bolt like I'm an ax murderer."

She reached into her pocket and pulled out the raisins that had not been consumed the night before. "Look, girls." They came running, falling over each other's backs to get at her. She kept her hand at thigh height, and they jumped for the raisins, like retrievers leaping for a Frisbee disk. Willow had never met chickens until she followed her asshat boyfriend to Vermont. And now she found them charming. But not charming enough to stay in Vermont forever.

Willow reached into her pocket again and offered more raisins.

"There's no way they're enjoying those half as much as I did."

Willow turned to meet Dane's smile. But then his grew a bit sad, and he turned toward the open barn door.

* * *

Dane waited while Willow fed her chickens, and then he followed her into the house, into a big old room with wide pine boards on the floor. At one end was the kitchen, and a thick-topped work table on turned legs. At the other end of the space was a living area, with an overstuffed sofa and comfortable chairs. It was the sort of room where happy lives were lived.

"Breakfast first or tow truck first?" Willow asked, shrugging off her coat.

"Definitely breakfast," he said. "I'm dying." He put his coat on an empty hook next to hers, and tried not to notice how right the two looked hanging there together.

"I'll bet you're hungry. Hey! I don't think I even lost power," Willow said. "That's a first." He watched as she put a hand to the side of her slow cooker, which sat on the counter. "Still warm," she mused. She went to the refrigerator and took out a bottle of orange juice.

"I'll pour," he said.

"Thanks." She opened a cupboard and slid two juice glasses onto the table in his direction.

"Now, coffee," she said, turning to a very fancy Italian machine with copper pulls.

"That's gorgeous," he said.

"It sure is," she agreed. "And it's not mine. He left this, the motorcycle and a room full of art books. At least the coffee machine is useful."

"Let's fire her up, then," he said. "Can I do it?"

She shrugged, flipping a piece of that silky hair over her shoulder. Without thinking, he reached out his hand and smoothed her hair down her back. She turned to smile at him, and he admired her lips again. "You can try, but it's a fussy machine. It took me months to get the shot size correct."

"I like a challenge," he said. He saw her keeping an eye on him as he mounded espresso grounds into the arm of the machine, then carefully tamped them down. "How am I doing?" he asked.

"You have some moves," she said.

"I think I proved that already," he said with a wink.

Willow blushed, and Dane dragged his eyes off her face. He had to stop flirting right this second. It wasn't fair to her. Never mind that he wanted to cup her sweet ass in his hands, and then back her over to that sofa on the other end of the room. He wasn't going to do that, or any of the other fun little plans his mind would hatch every five minutes until he got himself the hell away from her.

As much as he'd love to install himself in her kitchen, in her bed or in her life, there was no way he could do that. And flirting sure as hell wouldn't make leaving any easier. Instead, he was going to keep the conversation going nice and easy. After he'd called the tow truck, he would give her one friendly kiss and get the hell out of Dodge.

He chose a bar stool located safely across the worktable from her, watching while Willow flitted around her kitchen. She wore an endearing look of concentration, dashing between the stove and the refrigerator. He drank his espresso and thought how ordinary the whole scene should be.

But it wasn't, not for him. He would never have a home like this, with a companion an arm's length away frowning over the omelet pan. There was something about this girl and this room that drove that all home. Sober truths marched gloomily through his head. It happened sometimes, and he always managed to chase them away again.

Flying down the mountain at superhuman speed usually did the trick.

Dane didn't have time for a midlife crisis. The way he figured, his life expectancy was about forty-five years, and he'd be blotto for the last five of them. The time to have a midlife crisis was well past.

Now there was a cheery thought.

Willow put two toasted tortillas on a plate, then flipped three eggs on top. She finished with a swirl of hot chili. "*Et voilà*," she said, putting the plate in front of him. "There's about ten-million calories there. That should be enough to shore you up."

"Thank-you, oh great one," he said, and she grinned.

She made a smaller plate for herself and sat down opposite him.

"Have you ever skied?" he asked, taking a forkful. It was heaven. "This is great, by the way."

"Thanks. No skiing for me. Crazy—right? To move to Vermont, and not know how to ski."

"You could still learn."

"Maybe," she said. "But lift tickets are pricey. Then there's the gear. All your friends are skiers, I bet."

My friends. Right. "Well, some of them are snowboarders." That won him a smile. But Dane didn't have friends, he had competitors. He had drinking buddies, and the occasional fuck buddy. And none of those people knew him at all. Dane took another bite, and then tipped his head back in appreciation. "*God* this is good. You're quite a cook."

She beamed at him. "You'll have to thank The Girls for these eggs. They laid them for you this yesterday. Vermont's finest."

"How many of Vermont's finest do you get a day?"

"Just under one per chicken." She had a dot of chili on her cheek, and it was all he could do not to reach over and brush it away. He took another bite instead. "So, about twenty eggs. I sell them to the gourmet store in town."

"Does that pay well?" he asked.

"No. But every little bit helps. If I could just finish my doctorate, things would get easier."

"Doctorate in what?"

"Clinical psychology."

He put down his fork and laughed.

"What's so funny? Are you afraid of shrinks?"

"Hell yes."

"Well, I plan to work with kids. So you're safe with me."

I'm anything but, he reminded himself. "Why were you interested in that, anyway?"

She held his gaze for a long moment before answering. "It's complicated."

He nodded. So Willow had secrets of her own. Don't we all?

* * *

After breakfast, Willow called AAA with instructions as to where to find their two stuck vehicles. "The Jeep can probably be freed and driven away," she said. "The truck won't start at all." She listened, then thanked them and hung up.

"What did they say?" Dane asked from the sink, where he was doing the dishes.

"They'll get to us when they can. When I pressed, the guy said an hour. But he might have been blowing smoke up my ass."

Dane passed her a clean dish, which she dried on a towel. He had it again—the strange sensation of stepping momentarily into someone else's life—a life where there was breakfast with the girlfriend, a few dishes to wash and a second cup of coffee. He felt like he was watching a movie, and the star looked exactly like him.

"What?" she asked suddenly.

He must have been staring at her. Dane shook his head. "Nothing, sorry. Distracted."

She put down the towel. "Thanks for doing the dishes."

"Thanks for the awesome breakfast." He gave her a slow smile.

She jutted a thumb over her shoulder. "I'm just going to clean myself up a bit, since we have to wait," she said. "Make yourself at home," she said.

"You go ahead," he said. "Thanks."

He made himself turn away and refill his juice glass.

* * *

Dane heard the shower running, and he was briefly tortured by the image of Willow's naked body underneath the hot water. He shifted his weight on the bar stool to accommodate the bulge in his jeans.

Down, boy.

The shower sounds stopped, and he scanned yesterday's newspaper, blocking images of Willow undressed a couple of rooms away. The tow truck would come, and he'd be out of here, gone from here. He wouldn't see Willow again. That was the way it had to be. Always.

Then the phone rang. Dane waited, wondering if he should answer. If it was AAA calling, Willow would want to know what they said. After two rings, he picked up. "Hello?"

"Um…hello?" a woman's voice said. "Is Willow home?"

"Yes, she is," he said. "Let me call her for you."

But Willow came skidding into the kitchen then, tying a bathrobe around herself, her eyes wide. "Is it AAA?"

He shook his head. "That's what I was thinking, but…" he passed her the receiver.

"Hello? Hi, Callie! No…no need to alert the authorities." Her eyes flicked to his, amusement playing in them. "Long story. But he's, um, stuck in the snow on my road. Waiting for the tow truck. Right. No serial killers here."

Dane forced his gaze onto the same newspaper headlines he'd been staring at before. They were just as engrossing with Willow in a thin bathrobe as they'd been while she showered.

"So will I see you for yoga this week?" she asked. "No way! How come you're *always* the one on call? I know. Okay. Text me." She hung up the phone. "Sorry, my friend called to make sure I wasn't dead in a snowdrift. She worries about me out here alone."

"Should she?" he rubbed his shoulder, which was stiff from slumping onto the floor of his Jeep all night.

"No, but she's a doctor. They're born to worry. What's the matter with your shoulder?"

He shrugged. "It's fine."

She moved to stand behind him. "I knew you shouldn't have carried that fifty-pound bag." She put her hands onto his shoulder muscle, the heels digging in. "Knots," she said.

"Christ," he said. "You're strong for a little person."

"Who are you calling little?" she asked, pressing her hands even further into his deltoid. "I worked as a masseuse during college. Here, bend this arm onto the table." She shifted him, then went back to work on his shoulder.

"Holy..." The force of her touch was startling—all that power in a small package. Her hands moved up to the back of his neck, and he dropped his head forward. He could feel her body leaning against his, her stomach grazing his back. Thank God for the big pine tabletop in front of him. The tent he was raising in his jeans right now would probably be visible from space.

And she was clearly hitting on him. That made things even harder, so to speak.

Willow's hands spent a moment or two on his other shoulder, before working down his back, his traps, his lats. By the time she got down low, to where his waist met his bottom, he was holding his breath, his arousal complete. Her hands stilled, coming to rest lightly on his waist. They both held their breath; it was so quiet. If he turned around now, he would find her waiting for him.

Don't turn. Don't turn.

* * *

Willow watched him turn.

She hadn't reached for him—she made herself wait. And for a split second, she thought he didn't feel what she felt, that he would sit tight, facing the table. He could have, and it would have been an easy way to say, "No, thank-you."

But just as she was processing her disappointment, his broad shoulders swiveled, and he rotated on the bar stool, catching her hands in his, pulling her in. His lips claimed hers, and she watched his long lashes fall closed, felt his breath on her face. As he tightened her body against his chest, controlling the kiss, she felt his arousal, the swollen shaft pressing against her belly.

His mouth tasted of orange juice and longing.

Six

HEAVEN HELP HIM, but this girl was like kryptonite on his willpower.

Dane couldn't resist her mouth, his tongue making long draws on hers. Her hips fit into his hands, the fabric of the bathrobe thin enough that he could feel his fingers digging into her skin. He braced her body against his, her full breasts pressing against his chest.

She moaned very softly from the back of her throat, and the sound made his balls throb. Scooping his hands under her bottom, he pulled her up onto his knees, so that she straddled him on the stool. He fumbled for the knot on her bathrobe, giving the loose end one good yank. It fell open. God almighty, she was naked underneath.

Just once more, he reminded himself. *And then you will walk away.*

Their kisses heating up, he took both her breasts in her hands, all the while his cock punched against his jeans. He could take her right there on the bar stool. But Willow made him feel greedy in about a hundred different ways, and he'd get only this one chance with her. Dane wanted to lay her out and see every inch. "Willow," he said, his voice thick. "I want you in your bed."

Her teeth nipped his neck while she wrapped her legs carefully around him. "Then take me there."

He braced her in his arms and headed for the back of the house. The feel of her cradled against his chest was so foreign—and so intimate—that he didn't ever want to put her down. This must be what it felt like to belong to someone, to move together through the world.

Hello, asshole?

Where were all these pointless ideas coming from? Clearly Dane needed to fuck a little more and think a little less.

He carried her through a dark dining room. Beyond it lay a sliver of daylight. As Dane approached, he saw the quilted end of a bed. With four more strides he was there, depositing her gently on its surface, spilling open her robe, exposing her body to his eyes. She didn't cover herself. Instead, she watched his face as his gaze devoured her.

Dane pulled off his T-shirt, then dropped his jeans and his briefs in one motion. He knelt down beside her on the bed. He feasted on the sight of her at close range—those mounded breasts with rosy-pink nipples, feminine curves at her hips. Sliding onto the bed, he spread himself out on her body, covering her, touching every inch at once. She was smaller and softer than the ski team Amazons he usually consorted with. He smoothed her hair onto the sheet, dropping kisses into the curve of her neck.

He felt her hands reach around him, kneading and smoothing the muscles of his back. Then Willow's surprisingly strong hands moved down to grasp the muscles in his ass, stroking and rubbing him, her fingertips dropping to graze his balls until he groaned. His hips twitched with longing, but it was just dawning on him that he had a problem. "I want you so bad," he said, laying his hard shaft between her legs. "But I don't have another condom."

Willow looked up at him, cupping her hands to the back of his head, entangling her fingers in his hair. Then she bent her knees, squeezing his hips with her legs. "Kiss me," she gasped. And when he covered her mouth with his, she stroked him with her tongue, her hands braced against his back. He was so aroused, he thought he might just combust if she kept kissing him that way.

She broke off, saying, "I'm on the pill."

Dane closed his eyes and tried to think. Between her parted legs, he was all too conscious of the wetness there, slicking the base of his cock with her desire.

But rules were rules.

He shook his head. "I never go without a condom. I won't even use a different brand." Then he kissed her, his lips biting and tasting her lower lip.

It sure as hell wasn't personal.

Willow gave the most erotic sigh he had ever heard. "Well, there are many other lovely ways I can make you happy."

Dane slid down her body, his tongue on her neck, her breast. "I like the sound of that."

But first, he wanted to taste her.

He dragged his lips down to her hip bone, where his tongue did a lazy stroke. Then he slid his palm onto the sweet mound between her legs, and she whimpered, her thighs falling open to him.

Dane chuckled at the wanton pleasure of it all. Most mornings, he was at the gym, beating his muscles into submission or strapping on his slalom skis for three hours of drills. But in broad daylight he lay in this white bed, his face on the velvety skin of a beautiful woman. Maybe he could make her shout his name. At a slow pace designed to tease, he dragged his hand down, thumb sliding slyly into her folds, where the moisture waited.

She moaned, long and low.

He spread her legs gently, his mouth landing on her inner thigh. His lips spread wide, he sucked on her skin. With his thumb, he did a slow circle around her clit. Willow groaned, gripping the bed sheet with both hands.

Taking his sweet time, Dane nosed into her blond curls, and he felt her body contract with expectation. Then he slid two fingers inside her, while his tongue swept across her swollen sex.

She was panting now, her fingers reaching for him, brushing his ears, his shoulders, whatever she could reach. He flattened his tongue onto her, his fingers thrusting inside. She rolled her hips up to meet him, giving herself over to her desire. Every little noise she made, every whimper, every breath, turned him on. He wanted so badly to be a part of her, to bury himself inside her and never come out again. Dane heard himself groan with frustration.

"Please," she whispered. "Please."

Later, he would remember that her pleading was nonspecific. The request could have meant anything. But she was speaking to *him*, asking him for more. And he'd never wanted to give himself to anyone so badly in his life. The lure of the full experience—the beautiful girl, and the luxury of a morning in her kitchen, and then in her arms— was more than he could withstand. And then he was in motion, climbing her on sheer adrenaline. Hiking himself up onto her chest, with a single thrust he pushed his cock deep inside.

And holy… he caught his breath.

At once, his miscalculation was all too obvious. For a man whose goal in life was to feel almost nothing, he'd just thrust himself into heart-stopping moment. The wet velvet feel of her against his naked skin was so overwhelming that he froze, stilling himself, his face in her hair.

Deep POV

Willow whimpered again, her arousal taking over. Her hips rocked beneath him, and the sensation nearly shot him through the roof. Wet and warm, her body cradled him, held him, and it was like nothing he'd ever felt before.

He heard his own growling moan. He thrust his hips once, twice, the sensation knocking him to near oblivion. His own body was like a foreign country, driven by an unfamiliar yearning he didn't know he owned. Every inch of him was hypersensitive. He could feel the friction of her breasts against his chest, even her hands on his back seemed to burn him up. It was too much, and he felt himself breaking. He tensed for it—for the familiar sensation of climax. But that isn't what happened. It was something else, and it took Dane a moment to figure out what. *deep POV*

There were tears springing from the corners of his eyes. Actual tears. *his tears*

What the fuck?

His surprise was enough to wake up that part of Dane that was always intent on maintaining control of the situation. He pulled out quickly. And just as Willow opened her eyes in surprise, he rolled off her and onto his side, then turned her small body with two hands, until she was facing away from him. Holding her hips in his hands, he thrust upward again, entering her from behind.

And there it was again, that amazing feeling. Holy hell. She was like a path of honey; he could dip himself in and out forever and want nothing more. "Sweet, sweet thing," he choked out, his hips moving on their own volition.

His heart hammering, Dane reached a hand over Willow's hip and between her legs, flicking her clit with his thumb. She arched her back, leaning that sweet ass of hers into him with a gasp.

"Sweet, sweet," he whispered, his voice shaking.

Willow's body strained against him. "Oh, God," she said. "*Dane.*"

He bucked into her, flying high. He buried his face in her hair and thrust harder.

Willow grabbed his hand, pressing it down on her sex. As he rolled the heel of his hand onto her, she came hard, moaning and straining, her body squeezing his cock in an embrace. And then he couldn't hold on a moment longer. He burst into her, pouring himself into a woman's body for the first time. With his hand that was still clamped over her, he slammed her against his hips once, twice, three times, until finally he could rest.

Dane's heart thundered in his chest, and he sucked in air. Between his legs, he could feel Willow tight on him, her body still milking tiny contractions around his cock. He had never felt anything so beautiful. He panted into the nape of her neck, her hair sticking to his face, which was still wet from his tears.

Willow turned her chin toward him, tilting her shoulder as if to face him.

Dane clamped both of his arms around her. He curled one of his long legs over hers, holding her tight, but keeping her facing away. *Calm down*, he told himself. He stroked her breast and tried to measure out his breaths to slow himself.

Willow curled a hand around his and squeezed. The tears leaking from his eyes still came. He lay quietly, trying not to sniff.

It was just that he'd been up all night. It must be exhaustion breaking him down. Turning him into a total pussy.

He closed his eyes. With his hand on Willow's chest, he could feel her own breathing lengthen and slow. His body listening to hers, he finally began to relax.

* * *

Willow lay locked into his embrace wondering what had just happened.

She'd felt it again, an odd intensity between them, unfurling when they touched. And now he clung to her, like a drowning man to a life preserver. She closed her eyes, memorizing the feel of his powerful chest against her shoulders.

They fit together perfectly. *Deep POV*

Seven

DANE WOKE UP slowly, sunlight against his eyelids. As he came to, he realized that one of his arms was still curled around Willow's waist. The shock of waking up next to her sent his pulse racing.

Jesus, dude! What are you still doing here?

Blinking at the curve of her neck, it was cruelly apparent just how far he'd strayed from the plan. And he couldn't even count how many of his own rules he'd broken.

Go, asshole. Now.

Carefully, he eased his arm off of her body. Willow sighed in her sleep, rolling onto her stomach, her face still turned away from him.

His heart pounding, Dane counted to sixty. Then, he slid carefully off the bed. As noiselessly as possible, he gathered up his clothes, carrying them into the kitchen. There he speedily got dressed, put on his coat and boots and stepped outside.

The cold air greeted him, snow crunching under his feet. He sucked the chill into his lungs, and Vermont's piney scent began to do its work on him. Outdoors, under an open sky stretched between two mountain ranges, his life slid back into control.

He walked into Willow's garage. He found her snow shovel leaning against the door. *That's right, Dane. Time to dig your way out of this one.*

Carrying the shovel, he began to walk down her driveway. As he descended, he saw a tow truck lumbering along the road, slowing down as it approached.

Dane picked up his pace and ran to meet it.

* * *

Willow woke up alone.

Sitting up in her empty bed, she listened. The stillness of her house was so complete that she knew at once he was gone.

Easy, she cautioned herself. *Don't you dare be surprised.*

Still, there was no denying that she hoped he wasn't really gone. She dressed quickly. In the kitchen, he was nowhere to be found. There was no evidence he'd ever been there at all, save a single juice glass on the table and the raw feeling of her bitten lips.

Willow shrugged on her coat and began to look around for the keys to her truck, which she'd left on the table. But they were nowhere to be found. Just as she began to worry, she heard an engine. Out the kitchen window, she saw her truck pull up the drive and into the garage. A few seconds later, Dane emerged with her snow shovel, which he leaned against the side.

She stuffed her feet into her boots and clomped outside. "It started!" she said. "Oh, my God, thank-you so much."

He smiled, but his eyes didn't quite meet hers. "The tow truck pulled her out of the ditch," he said. "When I cleaned out the tail pipe, she started right up."

"And your Jeep?"

"I'm back in business." He gave her another smile, but accompanied by the same shifty gaze.

Oh no, her heart said.

"I'm so embarrassed that I slept through that," she said.

He shook his head. "It took no time at all," he said. "The guy was in and out."

Just like you're about to be, Willow thought. She felt her face get hot. "Did he leave me a bill?" she asked.

He waved off the question. "I took care of it." Then Dane stuck a hand in his pocket, jingling his keys. "I've got to get on the road now," he said. He took one step closer.

"Right," Willow whispered, crossing her arms on her chest, steeling herself for his rejection. He still would not look her in the eye. Instead, he took one more step, putting an arm around her shoulder. Then he kissed her.

"Mmm," she could not help but sigh. Even if his eyes said no, his mouth was warm and loving. He tasted her slowly. For a heart-stopping minute Willow wondered if he would come back inside.

But then he pulled back, whispering in her ear. "Goodbye, Willow."

She didn't trust herself to say anything. She could only hug herself with her arms as he finally met her eyes. They were as blue as the sky, and held hers for a long moment. Then, with what looked like reluctance, he turned his back and walked away.

Willow watched him start down the driveway at a walk, wondering if he'd turn around and wave. Instead, he accelerated into a run, long strides carrying him toward the road.

She went back into her kitchen, weighed down by her own disappointment.

Eight

DANE STEERED THE Jeep through the newly white world, across the Connecticut River and into New Hampshire. He took the curvy back roads after he left the highway. A sign on the shoulder read Moose Crossing, Next 3 Miles.

Liars. Dane made this fifty-mile trip once a week, and he had yet to spot a moose. He hadn't seen one since he was a kid, growing up in the Green Mountains. Back when his mother was alive, they used to go camping every summer, pitching a tent in the state park and violating the rules against campfires. His brother, Finn, would whistle as he built the fire, showing Dane how to use pine needles for tinder and demonstrating the importance of sufficient kindling.

Now Finn couldn't even get out of bed.

Dane tapped his fingers in time to the sounds of The Clash coming from his speakers and stretched back against the headrest. Alone, the Jeep humming along the road, he felt in control again. His body felt loose, with the telltale languor that was the result of intense sexual gratification. He could still feel the damp of Willow's body on him and a mild chafing where she'd stroked him.

His mind lingered on the feel of her hands on his stiff shoulder, the way she'd massaged him into complete arousal.

Christ. He was horny again. *Good re sexarousal*

He turned up the stereo volume and steered his thoughts to the busy days ahead.

* * *

When he pulled into the nursing home parking lot, it was one o'clock.

He stepped out of the Jeep, stretching his frame in the sunlight. The day after a blizzard nearly always featured this kind of perfect cloudless blue sky. Even with his shades on, it was hard to take. Nowhere on earth was Dane more aware of his own fragile mortality than on this particular property, where inside the building people lay bent and broken in a hundred different ways.

He'd learned on past trips that the fickle Gods of rural cell phone coverage smiled on this parking lot, and so Dane delayed the inevitable by calling Coach.

"Where are you?" Coach said quickly, always wary of Dane's disinclination to show up for flights on time.

"I'm going to be a day late," Dane said quickly. No point in beating around the bush. "Sorry, Coach. I'll catch a night flight, and be there in time for course inspection."

"Aw, kid. They're going to shoot me on sight," Coach complained, "when I turn up with more excuses for you."

"So take a later flight yourself. Or tell Coach Harvey to go fuck himself. Seriously."

"Where are you?"

"I just pulled into the nursing home. I'll be a couple of hours here, then I'll shoot down to Boston. I got the Jeep stuck last night and couldn't get dug out until midmorning. Honestly. Show Harvey a fucking newspaper. We got two feet, and Logan was shut down for a few hours. I heard it on the radio. I'll be there on time, and I'll ski fast. And then he can kiss both of our asses."

Coach sighed into the phone, and it sounded like a hurricane gale. "See that you do."

"Have a beer on me, Coach. I'll see you tomorrow."

"I have *too many* beers because of you, kid. If you would just *explain* to Harvey that you're having a family emergency...."

"No can do," he said. "But how about I just win the race, instead?"

"See you over there," Coach sighed. And then he hung up.

* * *

Dane tucked his phone away and walked into the home. He was greeted by the nauseating smell of floor polish mixed with antiseptic, and the glare of fluorescent lighting.

"Hello, Mr. Hollister," the receptionist called. "I have a letter for you from Dr. Brown." She held out an envelope.

That was not a good sign.

"Thank-you," he said, taking it. He gave her a salute and strode past, down the hall and to his brother's door. Pausing outside, he slid his finger under the flap and opened the envelope. The letter was just as discouraging as he assumed it would be. *Dear Mr. Hollister...still trying to get his infection under control. New antibiotics...haven't given up hope...*

Dane shoved the letter into his pocket and steeled himself before pressing the door open. His first view of

Finn was always a shock, and he'd learned to smile as a cover.

When he walked in, his brother's eyes flicked up to his from an unbelievably emaciated face. "Hey!" Dane said, taking three long steps toward the wheelchair, keeping eye contact like a champ. Even though Finn's chin sagged toward his chest, his brother's face contracted with a tic of recognition.

Or, maybe it was just a tic.

Dane couldn't be sure. The wall that the disease had built between them had started out low enough that it could be stepped across, if not ignored completely. But layer upon layer had grown these past fifteen years. Now it was so high as to be impenetrable.

"Hi, Finn." He took his brother's fragile hand into his and straightened it out as best he could. This hand, once incredibly strong and lithe, had helped Dane into his first ski boots, snapping the buckles into place. Now it was bent like a discarded piece of cardboard, cupped onto itself, useless.

And feverish.

Dane felt the pressure settling into his chest—the inescapable pain that always hung on him in this place. He looked around and found Finn's copy of the *Boston Globe*, unruffled, on the bedside table. "Let's find the sports section," he said, opening up the pages. "Who's on top of the basketball standings?" he asked. Then he began to read.

He read every article in the section out loud. Before Finn had deteriorated so far, Dane used to tell him things about his own life. His brother had given him drool-y smiles after hearing all of Dane's antics on the ski hill. But things were looking so desperate now, the feeding tube snaking out of Finn's blankets, the IV that delivered the newest antibiotic. It seemed unfair to talk about all the good things Dane enjoyed that Finn did not.

Or maybe he'd stopped telling Finn good news because talking to his brother felt too much like looking in the mirror. Now that Dane was knocking on thirty, his own unfortunate future loomed large. How long would it be before he was in Finn's shoes, perhaps in this very room? Dane had chosen this nursing home because it was the nicest he could find. At fifteen grand a month, it was expensive. But when Dane visited, his brother was always well cared for. He was clean and well tended, and the nurses who came through were cheerful and quite obviously well paid.

The best nursing home in New England. Now there was a dubious honor.

The sports section completed, Dane was fast running out of things to talk about. He watched Finn's eyes flicker across his face. There was still a person in there, paying attention. The disease had a marked effect on the sufferer's personality, but dementia didn't hit every victim the same way. He had no way of knowing how much his brother still understood, because the muscular deterioration had taken away his ability to speak more than a year ago.

Dane hesitated, wondering what to tell Finn next. *So, I met a girl.* Some part of Finn might still like to hear what his little brother was capable of pulling off in the back of a Jeep. But Dane wouldn't tell the story. Because if Finn were still able to understand it, then both of them would be depressed by the inevitable conclusion. Dane couldn't see the girl again because fate had determined that he would likely also be a loser in the same harsh game of genetic roulette.

Fate was a tricky bitch, anyway. Because if it weren't for Finn, Dane would have never met Willow. He would never be training in New England, and he wouldn't have crossed her path. Heads you win; tails I lose.

This kind of math—disease math—was always on his mind. How many years until his brain faltered, and he began to forget things? How many people would assume he was a drunk when his gait went goofy?

Lost in thought, he hadn't spoken in a couple of minutes. "Sorry," Dane said, his own voice echoing into the silence. "I'm shitty company today." He ruffled the newspaper again. "Let's see what's happening in the TV section. Maybe there's something good coming on for you this week."

Nine

"I REALLY APPRECIATE this favor, Willow." Her friend Travis swept his hand across his head again, trying to keep his wavy blond hair under control. "I really don't want to miss the big game." When he smiled, Travis's eyes crinkled at the edges. He had the open face and friendly gaze that a good bartender required.

"It's no problem, Trav," she said, tying the half apron around her waist. "I think it will be fun."

"Hope so," he said, looking up and down the bar, which was nearly empty, except for three ski-lift operators at the far end, and Willow's friend Callie at the other. "Wednesdays aren't too bad," he said. "And I'll be back before the bowling league guys come in. If there's something you can't find, ask Annie." He dropped his voice, even though the waitress was out of earshot in the adjacent dining room. "She's kind of a bitch, but she's worked here a long time."

"Gotcha," Willow said, smoothing the apron down. "Have fun and don't worry about a thing."

"If she gets slammed, I'll help out," Callie volunteered from her bar stool.

"If she gets slammed, I wanna watch," one of the lifties muttered, and his friends guffawed into their beers.

Travis leaned close to Willow's ear again. "They're disgusting, but probably harmless," he said.

"I've heard worse." She flashed him a smile.

When Travis went out, Willow did a little twirl in front of Callie. "This *is* kind of fun. Like playing lemonade stand, but with alcohol."

The waitress, Annie, came in from the dining room, slapping an order slip down on the bar.

Willow picked it up to read it. "Annie, I think this says: one book, one corn and a bird."

Annie snorted. "A Beck's, a Corona and a Budweiser."

"Huh, okay. Coming right up."

When Annie huffed out of the bar, Willow grinned at Callie. "See that? I get to say things like 'coming right up!'"

"I guess Travis asked the right girl for this favor." Callie sipped her beer. "Is he paying you for this gig?"

"I won't let him," Willow said. "He's helped me out a lot since John left. He recommended me for my temp job, he found someone to patch my roof for cheap. He's been a good friend."

"You know he wants you, right?"

Willow uncapped the Beck's and the Corona and looked up. "What?"

"Travis," Callie said. "He likes you. A lot."

Willow frowned, adding a wedge of lime to the Corona's bottleneck. The Bud was on tap, so she grabbed a pint glass off the rack and dispensed it with a flourish. "I don't see that."

"Then you're blind."

Willow set all the drinks on a tray and then leaned on the bar in front of Callie. "In other news, I had a small bit of luck last week."

"You mean, other than getting lucky?"

Willow put a finger to her lips. "Don't make me regret telling you about that, Callie. It's not a story I'd share with anyone else."

"We can't have drivers of Jeeps everywhere propositioning you."

"Right."

"Oh, Willow," Callie sighed. "I'm just jealous. I'm single for the first time in three years, and life at the hospital is all drudgery."

Willow reached across the bar and rubbed her arm. "I'm so sorry."

"Wait, I'm so busy whining I forgot to hear your lucky news."

"I rented out the apartment."

"Hurray!" Her friend applauded. "That's great. How?"

Willow shrugged. "I was going to make a new sign, but I got the call first. My new tenant is some kind of coach working at the mountain until spring. He was very apologetic that he only needed four months. And I'm jumping for joy, of course, just to have someone for that long."

"Is he hot?"

Willow smiled. "I'm happy to introduce you. He looks to be about sixty-five years old, but with a nice, friendly face."

Callie rolled her eyes. "Figures. But still, I'm so glad for you. That's a big relief, isn't it?"

"It will keep the bill collectors at bay. Maybe he can recommend another tenant by the time he goes."

Annie came into the bar again, with another of her illegible order slips. Willow hopped down to look at it before she could leave. "Does this say a White Russian? A Dirty Martini…and what's this last one?"

"A Shirley Temple."

"Right." Willow looked around, wondering why there weren't any cherries alongside the lemon and lime wedges that Travis had left for her. Where were the cherries? Willow squatted down to inspect the shelves below the bar. Travis had all manner of ingredients down here—Worcestershire sauce, different sorts of olives in jars. "My kingdom for a jar of cherries," she grumbled. "Who knew I could be undone by a Shirley Temple?"

"Wills?" Callie called her. "You have another customer."

"Just a sec…" Willow put the olives back onto the shelf and stood up quickly. There was now a man seated a couple of seats away from Callie.

Holy hell.

It was Dane. And he was every bit as surprised as she was, his bright blue eyes opening wide. Willow froze for a moment, her heart stuttering. She took a half step back, bumping into the beer cooler. Grabbing a tap to steady herself she accidentally dispensed a short stream of ale before righting herself. Her face began to flush to a deep red.

"Hi," he said, his eyes crinkling at the corners.

"Hi." She stared at him.

"You're not Travis," he said.

"Right." She cleared her throat. "I'm just covering for him so he can see his kid's peewee hockey game."

Their staring match was interrupted by one of the lifties. "Hey, hottie! Get down here a minute."

Willow wiped her hands on her apron. "And no good deed goes unpunished," she said. "Excuse me."

"I'm thirsty." The lifty waved her over. "Another Guinness, honey?"

"Coming right up," Willow sighed. At the taps, she began pulling a Guinness into a pint glass, tipping it carefully to avoid a head. "What can I get you?" she asked Dane over her shoulder.

"Um," he said. "I'd love a cheeseburger," he said.

"Food…" she said. "Tricky. Give me a minute." She took the Guinness down to the asshole at the end. Then she leaned over the bar to call into the next room. "Hey, Annie!"

A moment later the waitress appeared. "Where are my drinks?" she said by way of a greeting.

"Almost there," Willow promised. "Do you happen to know where Travis keeps the maraschino cherries?"

"Did you check the fridge?" she asked.

Willow felt herself flush again. Where was her brain? "As a matter of fact, I did not."

Annie snorted.

Willow leaned down for the bar refrigerator. "I thought they were indestructible," she said under her breath. "I think they found some at Pompeii. I'll have your cocktails in two shakes," she grabbed the cold jar of cherries. "Could you take a food order for this gentleman, please?" She nodded at Dane, as if he were a complete stranger. If he wanted to pretend their night together never happened, then that's what she'd do, too.

Annie lumbered over to him, jutting her boobs into his face. "The usual? Cheddar burger medium rare, onion rings and a Corona?"

"Great," Dane said, leaning back an inch or two.

To Willow, Annie said, "If I'm taking his food order, I'm going to put the beer under my number, too."

"Knock yourself out," she replied without looking up.

When Annie left, Callie spoke up. "I wonder if she delivers the food on those things, too?"

Willow heard Dane snort from behind the sports section.

She made a Shirley Temple, putting two cherries into the glass. "The kid will thank you for that," Callie said.

"Right?" Willow asked, trying to keep her cool. "That's the whole point of ordering a Shirley Temple. The cherry. So, why not an extra?" She put the drinks on a tray, then carried them down the empty expanse of bar. "It can be my signature drink. The Shirley Temple, with an extra cherry." Now she was babbling.

When Willow put the tray of drinks back down, the lifty nearest to her clamped a hand down on her wrist, trapping her there. "I'll take your cherry, honey," he said, leering up at her.

Her breath caught. Was there no end to this evening's humiliations? The asshole did not release his grip. As she stared the lifty down, there was a movement down the bar. From the corner of her eye, Willow saw Dane set down his newspaper and slowly push back his stool.

"It's a bad idea," Willow said, her voice steady, and her eyes narrowing at the dope across from her, "to be crude to the woman who controls your supply of beer."

Even as Dane moved closer to their little standoff, the lifty released her arm.

Feeling that she had something to prove, Willow didn't leap back just yet. "Now what do you say?" she pressed.

"Um, sorry? Can I have a refill?"

"I didn't hear the magic word," she said.

"Please?"

"That's better," she said, heading for the taps.

Silently, Dane reversed course, heading in the direction of the men's room.

Breathe, Willow, she told herself. Her heart was beating double time, and not because of the jerk who'd grabbed her arm. The sight of Dane had flustered her to the core. In the first place, he was about ten times as sexy as she remembered. It had been hard not to stare as he shrugged a red ski-team jacket off broad shoulders. And three or four days' growth of whiskers on his cut, masculine jaw made her want to reach over and measure the roughness with her fingers. She'd noticed him watching her, his intelligent eyes taking her in. The proximity was enough to drive her crazy.

For two weeks she'd been thinking about him. Sometimes she would remember the exact moment he'd first kissed her in the Jeep, and wherever she was—in the checkout line of the grocery store or sitting at the desk at her temp job—her eyes would go wide with disbelief. Images of him came to her unbidden. She'd picture his muscular chest hovering over her in bed and instantly go all squishy inside.

She hadn't missed the fact that he'd been prepared to yank the drunk off of her, either. He would do that for her. Yet he didn't want to see her again.

Why?

Willow shook her head. She poured two Buds for the lifties and tried not to be excited about seeing him tonight. *I'm not boyfriend material,* he'd said. But he'd said it *before* their amazing time together. And everything that happened after had been so electric.

Hope was a mean thing.

Callie waved Willow over. "The guy who ordered the burger—oh, my lord." She fanned herself. "Did you get a good look at him?"

Willow rubbed her forehead with both hands. "Why?" She had told Callie about the whole encounter— but she'd never said his name.

"Because I recognize him from the newspaper...shit. He's coming."

Willow pinched the fabric of her top and held it away from her body for a second. She was starting to sweat.

"You look frazzled," Callie said. "But I think you're doing fine. Except you forgot the guy's beer." She pointed at Dane.

"Oh!" Willow said, jumping toward the cooler. She grabbed a bottle out and uncapped it. "I'm so sorry," she said, managing not to look him in the eye. She would not give him the satisfaction of knowing how thoroughly their fifteen hours together had stirred her up.

"Not a problem," he muttered, "Thank-you."

She made herself turn away, scribbling the lifties' beer count onto Travis's clipboard.

"Willow!" Annie bellowed, setting a plate down in front of Dane. "You gave him the wrong beer. He drinks Corona."

Willow's pencil froze over the paper. Then she turned around slowly. It was with utter horror that she realized which bottle he held in his hand.

She'd brought him a Saint Pauli Girl.

Dane was watching her, amusement in his eyes. He held up a hand quickly. "It's fine," he said, taking a swig to prove it. "I like this one a lot."

"You're a terrible bartender, Willow," Annie said, hands on her ample hips.

"Why don't you say it a little louder, Annie," Willow snapped, her face flaming. "I don't think they heard you all the way in the back." She grabbed another order slip out of Annie's hand and walked away.

* * *

Dane watched Willow retreat to her friend's end of the bar. She was even more lovely than he remembered, her hair shining in the soft light of the bar. She wore a top that showed off her narrow shoulders, then flared softly over the top of her slim jeans.

"Callie, this handwriting is completely unintelligible," he heard Willow say. "I think Annie is doing this intentionally."

"Let me look," her friend said. "Pour me a refill, and I'll work on it."

Willow handed her friend the slip and dispensed a pint of UFO Pale Ale into her glass.

"The first one is a prescription for an antibiotic," Callie snorted. "This is worse than a lot of the things I see at the hospital. Actually, I think the first one says Apple Martini. The second one starts with an S. It could be Screwdriver. Or Scotch and Soda? No..."

As Dane watched, Willow plucked a Corona from the cooler. She popped the cap and shoved a lime in the top.

"What are some other drinks that start with S?" Callie asked.

Willow approached, putting the Corona down in front of him. She never raised her eyes to his.

"You didn't have to do that," Dane said quietly, but she'd already turned away, back to her friend.

So that was the way it was going to be. She wouldn't even make eye contact. But what could he really expect after that fuck-and-run he'd done? That was two weeks ago. He'd replayed the entire encounter in his mind a dozen times since. Now that he was back in the States for a little while, he'd taken care not to drive past her house on his way to the mountain. He didn't want to have to see the lights on inside, wondering what she was doing and whether she was alone.

It wasn't any of his goddamned business. And it never would be.

"Starts with an S...Sea Breeze?" Callie guessed. "Sidecar?" Even if Willow was doing everything she could to stay out of Dane's orbit, her friend did not pick up on it. "Do you know any?" she asked, looking right at Dane, trying to engage him in conversation.

His eyes flicked up at Willow before he answered. "Um, Southern Comfort?"

"7 and 7," Callie offered. "Sex on the Beach?"

"Sex in a Jeep," Dane said under his breath as Willow moved past him.

Apparently, he didn't say it quietly enough. Because Callie choked on her beer, and then began to sputter. She swiveled on her stool to stare at Dane.

Willow's eyes flashed as she stalked past him toward the lifties. She said something under her breath that might have been "shoot me."

Dane didn't even know why he'd said it. He hadn't meant to embarrass Willow, he only wanted her to look at him. But she wouldn't. And now her friend down the bar couldn't stop looking at him.

Smooth, Dane.

But he'd never been smooth, except while wearing a pair of skis. And in most of the places he went in a week, that was enough. Win enough races and people threw themselves at your feet, whether or not you lack social graces. He was all competence on the snow, and that's where he planned to live his life, until the moment his body failed him, and they carted him down on the goddamned ski patrol sled.

He felt a cold gust of air at his back, and moments later a bunch of men tromped into the bar carrying bowling bags. With her face the color of a beet, Willow began taking beer orders. And when Annie turned up looking for her cocktails, Willow handed the slip back to her. "Callie shot beer out of her nose, ruining this before I got a good look at it. I think it said Apple Martini and…"

"Sloe Gin Fizz," Annie scowled.

"I guess we didn't think of that one," Callie giggled.

Willow said, "With friends like you…" Then she reached for a bottle of sloe gin.

* * *

As the bar filled with people, Dane knew he should settle up and get the hell out. Watching Willow was sweet torture, because he couldn't have her, no matter what. Even so, he couldn't tear himself away. Though clearly outgunned, she poured beers and mixed drinks with grace and humor. Every guy in the bar snuck looks at her, hoping for a smile or a glance.

Dane's mother would have called her a "firecracker." That was her word for women with spirit. Even though she died almost fifteen years ago, his mother's favorite phrases had been coming back to him lately. So had Finn's. He missed the sound of his brother's voice.

"Sorry I'm late!" Travis called out, ducking under the bar. The relief on Willow's face was palpable. "The game went into overtime," he apologized. "Did everything go more or less okay?"

"It was amateur hour," Annie said, pulling two cocktails off the bar.

"It was amateur hour *and a half*," Willow corrected. "But nobody's bleeding," she crossed her arms over her chest. "These guys are settled up," she nodded at one set of bowlers. "They have a tab," she pointed at the other pack of guys. "The lifties owe you for six pints. Annie dropped Dane's check. That covers everyone except Callie." Willow grabbed a pint glass and began to pull a UFO.

"Nice job, Wills," Travis said. "Who's the UFO for?"

"For *me*, Trav," Willow said, exasperation in her voice.

"Good," he laughed. "I can't thank you enough." He looked at her the way the rest of the guys in the bar did, hungrily.

Dane had known Travis briefly in high school, before Dane had been shipped off to train at Burke Mountain. He'd been too much of a loner to keep in touch with people. But when Dane had begun showing up at Rupert's Bar and Grill for cheeseburgers and beer last month, Travis had made an effort to catch him up on the local gossip, including his own. The bartender had married his high school sweetheart and was now divorced.

And why wouldn't Travis put the moves on Willow? She was the brightest thing in the room. Probably the whole town.

Dane watched Travis work the room, checking in with his customers. He was the consummate bartender, always glad-handing, providing the punch line. He'd been the same way when they were teenagers. All charm, no substance. He chatted up the bowlers about their league, pouring a beer on the house for the high scorer. He was easy with people in a way that Dane never had been.

It was a low moment indeed to find himself jealous of Travis Rupert.

"So how's that man of yours, Callie?" Travis asked Willow's friend.

"Trav," Willow warned. "Not the question."

Travis's eyebrows shot up. "No?"

"I threw him out." Callie flushed. "Caught him…" she rolled her head back, eyes closed. "With a nurse. In an exam room."

"No shit," Travis said.

"And it's not bad enough that I'm living a cliché," she said. "I have to see them at the hospital. Every. Damned. Day."

"Callie, I'm so sorry," Travis said. He put one arm around Willow's shoulders and the other hand on Callie's. "What is it with you two and your luck?"

As Dane watched, Travis's fingers massaged the side of Willow's shoulder. And Dane felt an ache in his gut.

Time to leave.

Dane put cash into his check folder and shrugged on his coat.

"Where you been, Danger?" Travis asked suddenly. "I'd gotten used to seeing you parked at my bar." He bussed the empty burger plate.

"Austria." He drained his Corona, the lime stinging his lips.

"Did you make it onto the podium?"

"What do you think?" Dane zipped his jacket. "Good night, Travis," he said. He picked up his newspaper and then hesitated, "Good night, Willow."

She looked up, giving him a tiny nod. Then she ducked under the bar and maneuvered past the bowlers toward her friend.

Dane headed outside alone. The way he always did.

* * *

As soon as Willow went to sit with Callie, her friend grabbed her arm. "*That* was the Jeep guy? Oh, my GOD!"

"Shh…" Willow cautioned. "How mortifying."

"He's an Olympic champion, Wills. And *so* cocky, no?"

"You ladies know Dane?" Travis asked, removing Callie's empty beer glass.

"Not really," Willow said quickly.

"Good," Travis said, setting another beer in front of Callie. "That one is trouble."

"Why?" Callie asked, even though Willow kicked her foot under the bar.

Travis shook his head. "We went to high school together in Little Creek. The family is stark raving mad. Every last one of them. Like…institutionalized." He swept the bar mop across the pitted wood and moved away.

"He didn't look crazy," Callie whispered. "He looked hot." She giggled. "I thought you said he was just passing through?"

"Well he just did, didn't he?" Willow asked.

Callie whipped out her phone. "Let's look him up on Google."

"Let's not."

"Oh, come on, Wills! Maybe you'll see him again. You could wear that ski team jacket over your naked body."

Willow laughed. "It's not happening, okay? He made that very clear. If I try to imagine otherwise, it just makes me pathetic."

"You are not pathetic, Willow."

"Thanks, Callie."

Actually, there *was* something interesting about Dane's team jacket. Her new tenant had the same one. There must be some connection. If Dane had sent the coach her way, it really was a solid thing to have done.

Not that he seemed to want any credit.

Ten

ROMANTIC FAILURES ASIDE, Willow began to feel as if life was on an upswing. Now that her finances weren't so tight, she took care of all the little things that had gone slack. She got her truck's oil changed and stocked up on groceries. In the pharmacy, she treated herself to a new bottle of moisturizer—Vermont winters were shockingly drying. Then she went to the pharmacy counter and refilled her birth control prescription.

It was while she waited for the young woman in the white lab coat to staple the little white paper bag together that Willow began to worry. By her calculations, she ought to be having her period right now.

She went outside with her purchase and sat behind the wheel of her truck, her mind in a whirl. She'd forgotten to refill her last pack until a few days after what should have been the starting date. So, she'd skipped a few pills. With her long-term boyfriend gone from her life, it hadn't seemed important. Then she'd refilled it and taken the whole pack in the usual manner.

And some time in the middle there, she'd met Dane.

Willow began to sweat. She went back into the store and—for the first time in her life—bought a pregnancy test. With shaking fingers, she fumbled her way through the self-checkout kiosk instructions.

It was probably nothing, she reasoned on the drive home. The delay might have convinced her body to start her period late.

But ten minutes later, Willow was sitting on her toilet, staring at a positive pregnancy test.

There was only one person to call. "Callie?"

"Willow?"

"Please tell me you're not on call tonight."

"Why, sweetie? You sound upset."

"Can you come over? I need to see you."

"You're scaring me. Is this a problem that can be solved with ice cream? Or tequila?"

Willow blew out a breath. "Ice cream, I guess." *Definitely not tequila.*

"I'll come after work."

* * *

She and Callie sat on Willow's sofa, tears drying on both their faces.

"Oh, Willow. You have to stop beating yourself up over this."

"If there were anyone else to blame, I'd happily share," she said. "But this one is really on me."

"But blaming yourself just won't help. Besides, maybe the dude has special ski sperm. It made a beeline for your cervix."

When Willow laughed, a few more tears spilled from her eyes. "Just think what an excellent school psychologist I'll be some day. They can send all the knocked-up teenagers to my office door. And I'll know just what they're going through."

Callie laughed, wiping her eyes. "Oh, Willow."

"I'm going to leave a bowl of condoms out on my desk, the way some people offer candy."

"After everything else…I can't believe this is happening to you."

"It's my fault, Callie. Just like everything else that's gone wrong."

"I'm not going to ask you what you've decided to do. Because I hope you haven't decided yet."

Willow shook her head. "I have to sit with it for a little while, don't I?"

"Are you going to tell him?"

She blew out a breath. "I probably have to, right? But he won't take it well. I never met anybody less interested in commitment than this guy."

Callie groaned. "So that won't be a fun conversation."

"No," Willow sighed. "It won't be."

"You always said you wanted children, Willow."

"I do," she said softly. "Absolutely."

Callie's voice was small. "But the circumstances stink. This is a tough one, isn't it?"

"The toughest," Willow agreed.

"You'd be a great mother," Callie said as she stepped outside. "I just know it."

* * *

After Callie left, the last words her friend had said to her echoed through her brain. *You'd be a great mother, Willow.* At any other point in her life, she would have agreed. In fact, she'd always looked forward to having a chance to prove it. Her own parents had given her up in favor of drugs and alcohol. Willow had gone into foster care at age four, and then spent her elementary school years wondering what she'd done to make them abandon her. It had turned her into the world's most conscientious girl, the sort who was careful to get an A on every spelling test and to always wash the dishes before her foster mom could get to them.

It wasn't until college that Willow was able to put any of it in perspective. Once she discovered psychology courses, she was hooked. Right there inside her weighty hardcover textbooks she began to understand that her childhood behavior was a classic case of overcompensation. It was a relief to learn that there were simple explanations for the choices she made, and for the compulsion she always felt toward pleasing people.

Willow had looked forward to motherhood, to loving a child so much better than her own parents had done. But now she wondered if she was just overcompensating again. Would it be fair to the child to be born like this—to someone who had managed her life so badly that keeping food on the table would be a struggle?

She just didn't know. And now she had to sort it out herself, without the help of the loving partner she'd always imagined would go along with the fantasy of becoming someone's mom.

And soon.

Eleven

DANE WIPED THE sweat off his forehead with the arm of his jacket.

"I moved the seventh gate," Coach said. "The new combination is hairpins into flush. Can you see it from here?"

"Sure," Dane answered, pulling his goggles down. "I'll have to trim my line to the left in order to make the eighth one."

"Exactly. Whenever you're ready," Coach said, planting his poles in the snow. Then he skied down the side of the course, arriving at the finish line with a wave.

Slalom was not Dane's favorite. It was too fiddly, too technical for his taste. But a couple of times a season, he made it onto the podium in slalom nonetheless. Dane stood there at the top of the course, mapping it out one more time with his eyes. Then he launched himself forward, picking up speed into the first combination.

Even though slalom wasn't as fast and furious as his favorite events, he still enjoyed the *swish-swish* of his skis on the course and the *click-click* of the gates as he swatted past them. And there was nothing like a slalom run for emptying your mind of everything but the course and the moment. A distracted skier will clip a gate faster than you can say "disqualified."

He ran the first part of the course effortlessly, including Coach's hairpin change up. Things were still looking good on the steepest part, where Coach had set three tight combinations back to back. Dane began to lean

97

into the last third of the course, willing his quadriceps to keep up the good work. But the lactic acid buildup was starting to smart as he dove for the last half dozen gates.

The course was nearly in the bag when he felt his left foot slip. Looking down, that last fractional second, he saw his ski hook a gate, sending him skidding to the side. Dane's heart began to pound as he slowed down his speed, bypassing the last few gates and pulling up beside Coach with a hockey stop.

"What the fuck?" Dane asked, out of breath. He rubbed his left thigh.

"You caught a little edge there," Coach said mildly.

"I didn't feel anything grab the tip," Dane spat. "That was just odd." His heart rate refused to subside. He shook out his left leg, wondering what had just happened. *Muscle tremor*, his subconscious threatened.

"It's not at all odd," Coach said, his voice a warning. "Let's eat lunch. It's high time."

Dane gazed back up toward the course, as if the answers lay there. He massaged his left leg, trying to convince himself that nothing peculiar had just happened to him. *Move on*, he ordered himself. He pulled off his helmet, letting the cold air work on his sweaty head. "Okay. The main lodge or the scary pizza?" he asked. The trouble with ski mountain food was that it all sucked. It was overpriced and poor quality. Greasy soups, floppy pizza. Dane lived on it.

"Do you want to come to my place for lunch? I have pulled pork sandwiches."

"Really?" Dane asked. "I never saw you cook anything that wasn't a frozen dinner."

Coach chuckled. "I don't. But my landlady does. She brought a Tupperware container to my door, because she said the recipe made too much."

Uh oh. "Well that's a good deal for you," Dane said.

"Truly. You should meet this one, Dane. She's gorgeous. Get yourself a girlfriend for once."

Dane bent over to unbuckle his boots. "That's the thing, Coach. I don't have girlfriends. And, unfortunately, I can't really drop by your place unless she's not home."

Coach was silent for a moment, and when Dane stood up again, he snorted. "Really?"

"Yes, really."

He shook his head. "We've been in this town for about ten minutes, and you've already blown this girl off?"

Dane shrugged. "It's what I do."

Coach waited for Dane to pick up his skis. "Well, let's eat. I'm having a pulled pork sandwich. You can either come with me or not."

"If I see that truck in her driveway, I'm driving on by."

"You do that." Coach shook his head.

* * *

Willow had a temp job in town at the insurance agency. Several days a week she put on office clothes and helped the local agents renew policies and process claims. Like everything else in Willow's life, the job flickered like a candle in the wind—always on the verge of going out. This week, they'd only asked her in for three half days.

So it was just past one when she pulled into her driveway, spotting a familiar green Jeep parked at the top of the rise. Her first reaction was: *men are so freaking predictable.*

To say that her gift of food was calculated to summon Dane to her door was not strictly true. She'd braised a seven-pound pork shoulder to take to her book club last night, but then the women had eaten far less than she'd brought. And while Willow loved pulled pork, she knew she'd get sick of it quickly enough. Handing some off to Coach was not only sensible, but neighborly.

But she *had* wondered if he'd share.

So Willow gave herself points for intuition. But now that Dane was here, mere steps from her door, she knew she wasn't ready to tell him about the pregnancy. The news—the problem—was still too raw, too fresh. And since she already knew just how Dane would feel about it, Willow couldn't tell him until she knew precisely how she felt about it herself.

At least, as precisely as possible for someone as confused as she was.

She hopped out of her truck and sped inside. She wouldn't put herself in his path; she wasn't ready. But now that she knew Coach and Dane were a pair, at least she had a way to get in touch with him when she needed to—and not merely with barbecue. When she was ready to tell Dane, the nice older guy with the friendly eyes could be counted on to help summon him. She was sure of it.

In her kitchen, Willow put a crock of dried beans to soak on the table. She would make a batch of white bean chili tomorrow with green chilies and ground turkey. Chili was the perfect single girl food—beans were cheap and healthy, and when you got tired of it, you could freeze the rest.

She wondered if the spicy foods she liked to eat would start to put her off. Morning sickness—when did that start happening?

Her phone rang.

Twelve

THE PULLED PORK sandwich was remarkably tasty, just as Dane knew it would be. And Coach's little apartment was, as a chick would say, cozy. There were thick old wooden beams on the ceiling and a wood stove in the corner.

"Do you hear that?" Coach asked with a wink, as the sound of Willow's truck roared up the steep drive.

"Sure do," Dane sighed. "There's nothing I've ever done wrong that I wasn't immediately busted for. Remind me never to knock over a liquor store."

Coach laughed. "If things are as bad as you say, she won't knock. Does she even know your car?"

"Yeah." *Does she ever.*

Coach ate the last bite of his sandwich. "Someday, I'm going to dance at your wedding, kid."

Dane's eyes cut to his. "No way."

The older man nodded. "I know you think it's impossible. And God only knows who the bride will be. But someday...."

Something about Coach's words hit a little too close to home. He'd said *impossible* instead of *unlikely*, and Dane wondered why. He had never told anyone his secret. Of course Coach knew Finn was dying, but Dane had never told him the cause. He didn't need anyone looking up his own likely prognosis on Google.

He stood up and carried his plate over to Coach's sink, turning on the faucet. "Let's get back. And don't even *think* of abandoning me out there." He tipped his head toward the driveway. "I expect you to put on the bad cop routine. 'Danger, we're late for practice.'"

Coach guffawed. "Fine. I'll crack the whip."

"I'd really like to run some GS drills for the afternoon. If that's okay with you," Dane said. Just as he turned toward the door, there was a knock. "Christ," Dane said under his breath.

Coach only grinned, moving past him to open the door.

When the door opened, Willow stood there, her face serious, her eyes cutting from Coach to Dane.

Come on, girl. Don't be like this, Dane thought, uncharitably.

"Sorry, guys." She cleared her throat. "There's a call on my line from a nursing home in New Hampshire, asking for either of you. They said my number is on Coach's voicemail message?"

Oh.

Oh, Christ, no. Dane felt the floor tilt under him.

"Dane." Coach was watching him, his face stony. "They must have tried our cells," he said in a quiet voice.

But Dane only half heard him. He walked, zombie-like, out the apartment door.

"The phone is on the kitchen counter," Willow said as he passed her.

In Willow's kitchen, he raised the phone to his ear. "Hello. This is Dane."

"Mr. Hollister, this is Janice, one of the hospice..."

"I know who you are," he said, his voice unnecessarily cold even to his own ears.

"I'm so sorry to have to tell you this," she said. "But Finn has passed."

Brother dies

"Thank-you for calling," he said, with all the warmth of a robot.

"There will be arrangements to make…" she began.

"I'll call later," he bit out, then shut off the phone. He dropped it onto the table, wanting to break something—the phone, the table, his own head. Something.

He always knew this call would come. But he'd dreaded it anyway. Now he was well and truly alone. Very few people had ever loved Dane. There was Finn and his mother. And now they were both gone. Finn's body might even be lying in a refrigerator by now. Cold as ice.

Where Dane would be someday relatively soon.

He shivered.

* * *

Willow and Coach looked at each other for an awkward moment.

"It's…" Coach said. He took the cap off his head.

"…his brother," Willow whispered.

Coach's eyes widened, obviously surprised that Willow knew. "Yeah." He looked up at the ceiling, and then back at Willow. "Sorry about the call. I haven't rung up the phone company to get a phone line put in. Seems like kind of a waste…."

"No trouble," Willow whispered.

"So…I doubt we're skiing again today," Coach said. "Tell Dane I'm here, if he wants to talk."

"I will." She left him alone in the apartment and walked toward her own door. She stood there on her stoop for a moment, to give Dane privacy on his call. But there were no sounds coming from inside her kitchen. All she could hear was the excited caw of a hen who had just laid an egg. She pulled the kitchen door open, and saw Dane standing there by the table, the phone abandoned on its surface. He stared down at the wood grain, his eyes unfocused.

Willow tiptoed inside. His stillness was statue-like, his handsome face carved as if in concentration on something she could neither see nor hear. He didn't move, didn't seem to sense her. "Dane," she whispered, stepping forward. She put a hand on his shoulder. "Did you lose him?"

For a moment she was unsure whether he even heard her. Then he put his long hands on the table and bent forward, hanging his head. "I lost him a long time ago," he whispered hoarsely.

The pain in his voice gutted her. Willow put a hand on the back of his neck, her palm to his warm skin. "I'm so sorry," she whispered. "I'm just so sorry." She moved her hand to his back, rubbing it quickly—a chaste touch meant to shore him up. Whenever friends experienced grief, Willow always felt so helpless, and in spite of her terrifying complication with Dane, this moment was no different.

"He didn't see forty," Dane whispered. "Not even forty."

Willow watched his expression, but he did not look up at her. He seemed trapped in his own grief, as if in shock. She was about to ask him if she should fetch Coach, when he turned his head. Dane's eyes focused on hers. "What will I do without him?" he asked.

"Oh," she said, feeling her eyes mist. "I'm so sorry." He looked *lost*. She reached for him with both hands.

Dane stood up and wrapped his arms around her. He pulled her in tight, her chin tucked against his chest, her back held tightly by one big hand.

There was nothing she could say that would make it any better. She looped her hands behind his back and closed her eyes. She inhaled the scent of him—his wool sweater smelled like mountain air and wood smoke. His body was unbelievably sturdy.

But even the strong could ache.

Above her, Dane put his nose in her hair and breathed in. She hugged him a little tighter, and they stood there. The only sounds she could hear were their own breathing and the insistent call of a chickadee outside her window.

"Willow," he said after awhile.

She pulled back and looked up into his face. "What?"

He was there with her in the room then—not somewhere far away, as he'd been before. His long lashes blinked, his expression serious. "Why are you good to me?"

The question startled her. "You mean...right now?"

He nodded.

"Because...because..." she swallowed. *Because that's what people do.* "Because you're sad," she said instead.

Dane stared at her, as if considering her answer. She felt him begin to tremble, and it tore at her heart. She stepped close and squeezed him tightly again. He put his nose against her cheek.

"Dane," she said, softly, "is there someone I can call for you?" He'd said he'd grown up somewhere nearby. There must be other family members who needed to be told. Or a friend who could comfort him.

He leaned back again, regarding her with those lake blue eyes. "Not a soul," he said, his voice hoarse. Then he leaned forward and kissed her.

When his soft lips met her own, Willow went very still with surprise. He kissed her again, harder, this time. He tucked her hips against his own, and parted her lips with his tongue. She gasped against him, giving in to it. Desire flooded Willow as they kissed, sliding down her core, making rational thought difficult.

Her stomach fluttered. She shouldn't let him kiss her—there were complications between them that he didn't even know yet. It wasn't fair. But even as she had these thoughts, his mouth grew rough and needy. One of his hands raked her hair; the other clamped her body tightly to his. He cupped her bottom, pulling her against the hard evidence of his need, straining behind his fly.

There were a hundred reasons why this was a bad idea. But Willow's body was ready to overrule them. Her nipples hardened against his chest. She felt his thumbs at her belly, his hands grasping the fabric of the skirt she'd worn to work.

And his mouth—his beautiful mouth—was already making love to hers. He was hungry for her in a way that proved she hadn't been the only one thinking about their recent tryst.

"Willow," he rasped. "I want you to take it all away for me. Like you did before."

The psychologist inside her put in an appearance then. With a deep breath, she put both her hands on his face, but pulled her body back. Her voice was soft though her words were very clear. "Oh, honey," she said, and his eyes fell closed, as if the endearment was too much for him. "That doesn't really work."

His eyes snapped open again. "But it's all I've got."

"Shhh…" she smoothed her thumbs across his cheekbones.

He stepped closer to her. "Just make me forget."

The request was so raw, so honest that it squeezed her heart. She kissed him then, her mouth giving in to his need. His tongue responded with the urgency of someone lost, his mouth hot with desperation.

Whether or not it was a bad idea, Willow's body continued to oblige. Each brush of his roaming hands—against her breasts, her hips, cupping her bottom—charged her like a spark.

Dane released her, grabbing his own fly and ripping it open, shoving down his pants. His cock stood at attention, thick and veined, and pointing at her. Willow's breath caught at the sight, she felt herself flush. Dane leaned against her table as she grasped his shaft. With one glance up into his cool eyes, she lowered her mouth to his tip, kissing him gently on the knob. Then she began to lick him, and he groaned as she held him firmly in her hand.

She opened her mouth and slid him inside. Above her Dane braced himself against the table with a sigh. She felt one of his big hands slide over her hair. Willow took her time with him, her tongue stroking the length of him. Then she did her best to take as much of him in as she could.

Even so, Dane slipped a hand under her chin and gave a gentle tug. She stood up, startled, facing him. Dane pulled her in, his forehead against hers, their noses touching. "I need to see your face," he said.

Willow felt herself shiver at his words. That was her weakness, wasn't it? The handsome man said he needed her, and she came running. It never ended well, because it was always a lie.

Dane tugged on her skirt, a look of smoldering intensity in his eye.

For a long moment, she didn't move, only held his gaze. Then, deciding, she reached around to the back and unzipped the skirt herself, which fell to the floor. He put his hands on her hips, scraping her tights down her thighs. Then Dane slipped one arm under her butt and lifted her up, turning around to deposit her on the high kitchen table. With one good yank, he pulled her tights off and dropped them, leaving her naked from the waist down.

She held his gaze as he spread her knees. Willow put her hands on his shoulders, then wrapped her legs behind him. He held her bottom, balancing her on the edge of the table.

She couldn't look away.

Dane's eyes were still locked on hers as his thumb began to stroke her. Her eyes flickered as she felt herself flood with wetness. But his groan brought her back into the moment.

And then Willow found she could not break their gaze as his cool eyes bored into hers. She felt him breech her opening. And then it was her turn to groan as he worked into her completely. Their foreheads together, they rested there a moment, joined and silent. Willow held her breath.

Dane began to kiss her as he moved. "What is it about you?" he whispered. Then he covered her mouth with his. His thrusts grew more insistent, the pace fast and needy.

In spite of everything, Willow felt at peace, surrendering to his need. With his blue eyes on hers, it didn't matter that his grief was only beginning or that her pregnancy terrified her. Because sometimes, a moment of grace meant everything. The friction of his powerful body against hers began to break apart her thoughts, which became as wispy and dreamlike as wood smoke in the winter air.

"Oh, what you do to me," he panted. The sound of his arousal sunk right into her, bringing a moan from her chest into his ear. The edges of her vision began to darken, and when she felt his first shudder, she was right there waiting, squeezing his hips between her knees. His name escaped from her lips as climax overtook them both.

He cried out loud as he thrust one more time, and the sound of it nearly broke her heart. Her body squeezed his, as if to wring his pain away.

Breathing heavily, they clung together, unmoving. For several minutes it was peaceful. His fingers skimmed her back with an absent touch. Willow smoothed down his hair, gently massaging his neck. "You're going to be okay," she said eventually. She slid her chin off his shoulder and kissed him. "You're going to be fine."

He pulled back suddenly, staring, his face creased with pain. For a moment she thought he might cry. But then he shook his head fiercely. "I…I'm not, Willow," he said.

When he backed away from her, Willow lost her balance on the edge of the table, sliding quickly to the floor. "What's the matter?" she asked.

But by then, he was yanking up his pants. "This can't happen anymore." He zipped himself together. "This has to end."

"Dane, it was you who…"

He grabbed his jacket off the floor. "This is toxic. *I'm* toxic."

At once she was angry and embarrassed. "Who would *say* that?" She heard the anguish in her own voice as she scooped up her skirt, holding it in front of her nakedness.

"I guess I would." He turned abruptly for the door.

Willow watched him go, stunned by the sudden departure. There was no apology. He didn't even say goodbye.

Her door slammed behind him.

She still stood there, frozen, as she heard the engine in his Jeep roar to life, and then the sound of his tires kicking up gravel as he sped down her driveway.

When it sunk in that he was really gone, Willow gathered up her clothes and marched to the back of the house. With shaking hands, she plugged the old claw-foot tub and began to run a bath for herself. She stepped inside well before the water level was high enough. But he'd left her feeling dirty, and she could not wait to bathe.

She breathed in the steamy air and tried not to cry. Good grief. She ought to have known better. What did she really expect from someone grieving? No—not even grieving. He was still in shock. Here she had made the same mistake she always made—giving her heart to someone who wasn't capable of loving her.

Again, you idiot! When will you learn?

Willow tipped her head back against the edge of the tub and let the tears come. Maybe he'd even done her a favor. She knew now not to expect anything from him. It would be simpler to tell him she was pregnant after that forceful reminder of just how little he cared.

Thirteen

IT WAS WITH great reluctance that Dane steered his Jeep up Willow's driveway a few days later. He winced to see her truck parked in the garage.

He and Coach were headed to Boston's Logan airport again. And now that Finn was gone, there was no need to stop at the nursing home. He had tried to come up with an itinerary that did not involve picking Coach up here. But since Dane's equipment wouldn't fit into the sedan—and he really didn't feel like giving Coach a lot of explanation—he would just try to get his coach into the car without delay.

Dane got out of the Jeep and hustled toward Coach's door. "Hey, Coach," he said, opening the door and stepping into the living room.

"Hey, kid," Coach called, wheeling a duffel out of the little bedroom. "How are you feeling today?"

Because of Finn's death, Coach had suggested skipping the Italian race entirely. But then Dane would lose out on the World Cup points, which he did not want to do. And anyway, where was the sense in hanging around his seedy room in Hamilton, thinking dark thoughts?

When in doubt, fly down a mountain.

"I'm good. Let's go win some points."

Coach looked at his watch. "Excellent. We'll even have time to grab some dinner at the airport." Dane could feel him trying not to be relieved that they'd arrive together in Italy on time.

Dane picked up Coach's duffel and carried it outside. A flick of his eyes toward Willow's house detected movement inside. *Please stay in there,* he thought. *For both our sakes.* Dane could not be in the same room with that girl. Never again. He didn't know what it was about her, but whatever it was, she messed with his head. She made him want things—and do things—that were off limits.

No matter what, he could not let that happen again.

"Hey, Coach?" he asked, slamming the tailgate. "After we come back from this race, I think we can pull out of here. We'll find some hovel in the Alps and give our jet lag a break for the rest of the European tour." The next six weeks were chock-full of contests on the continent.

Coach looked at him sideways. "I wasn't going to rush you. I thought after you buried your brother we could talk about it."

Dane nodded. "But I'm not doing a funeral."

"No? I can put on a suit."

"We don't have family," Dane said. "There's really no point."

He watched Coach wrestle with the idea of making a suggestion or letting it go. "Dane," he began.

C'mon, Coach, couldn't you let it go?

"You might regret not saying goodbye."

Dane shook his head. "I said goodbye a long time ago."

Coach worked his jaw. "All right. Give me five minutes? I've got to hit the head. Then we'll go." He walked away.

Christ.

Dane decided to wait in the Jeep.

* * *

Willow hadn't panicked when the green Jeep climbed her driveway. But it quickly became apparent that Coach and Dane were going on a trip. The back of the Jeep was full of ski bags and luggage. Willow did the math. With the next dozen races in Europe (thank-you, Google), who knew when he would be back?

She dreaded telling him, but it had to be done.

Through the window, Willow watched Coach walk away. Her knees felt wobbly, but it was now or never. Without bothering to put on a jacket, she went outside and circled the Jeep.

She saw Dane watching her approach from the driver's seat, where he sat with the door open. "Hi," he said warily.

"Hi," she said, her voice squeaking.

"About the other day…"

She held up a hand to silence him. "Forget the other day," she said. "There's something else I need to say." She watched his face, but it revealed nothing. His face wore the same watchful, intense expression that she'd loved. There was no way he anticipated the bomb she was about to drop.

Willow cleared her throat. "I know you don't need this right now, and I wouldn't go there if I was sure I'd see you again…"

He didn't say anything.

"…and there's no easy way to say it." Her throat clenched. "But I'm pregnant. And I thought you'd want me to tell you."

She watched him take it in, expecting a flare of anger and surprise. But instead, all the light went out of his eyes.

His expression flat, his jaw hardened into a clench. "It can't be mine," he said finally.

"It is, Dane," she swallowed. "I'm sorry, and I don't want you to feel…"

"That's *not possible,*" he whispered. "You told me you were on birth control."

"I… I made a mistake." The flat expression on his face was almost scarier than if he'd started yelling. "I lapsed a little…" She was too rattled to defend herself further. She could only stand there, quivering from stress.

"Fine. I'll overlook the fact that you lied to me. But I need you to *think*, Willow." He licked his lips. "There must be someone else."

"There *isn't*," she said, trying to stand up for herself. "I know you aren't happy about this, but there's no chance I'm wrong."

He hung his head, and she almost missed the next words. "You can not have my baby."

"What?" she asked, even though she was pretty sure she understood.

"You can't. Because I…" his gaze came up to hers, and it was ice cold. "It's a bad idea to have this baby. Tell me you're not going to."

Willow's mouth went dry. This was so much worse than she'd even anticipated. Of all the disappointed things she'd imagined he might say, she hadn't come close to guessing that he'd push her toward abortion. But weirdly, his callousness helped. Because Willow saw it for what it was. A girl couldn't study psychology for seven years and not hear the truth through the noise.

This isn't about me.

The realization made it easier for her to survive the next sixty seconds. She dug her fingers into her palms.

"Dane, I'm sorry for my failure. I wasn't trying to lie about the birth control. I just didn't think the universe would be that cruel."

What he did next surprised her again. He actually laughed, but the sound was bitter, and his face took on a look of disgust. "Willow, make no mistake. The universe is *very* cruel."

Watching him, she'd forgotten to breathe. Now she sucked in air, taking a step backward. "I see," she said. It would have been easy to start screaming at him then, to tell him exactly what she thought of his coldness. But that would only prolong their encounter. Whatever baggage Dane carried—and it must be considerable—she wouldn't add to it. The right thing to do was to tell the truth, then take her leave. "I'm sorry. But what I've told you is true. And I don't know what you…" She took a deep breath. "I think you're better than this."

He swallowed roughly. "Then I guess you really are a fuck-up."

Okay, we're done here, she told herself, beginning to walk away.

"I'm not kidding. You can't have this baby."

She turned her back and accelerated toward her house. She would promise nothing. This really would be all her own decision.

"Hey! We're still talking, here!" he called after her.

Willow made it all the way back inside her kitchen before she started to cry.

* * *

"Is there a problem?" Coach asked, when he got into the Jeep.

"No," Dane said, staring into the distance over the steering wheel. He already had the engine running.

"I thought I heard shouting." Coach pulled his door closed.

"I didn't hear a thing," Dane said. He reversed the Jeep in an arc so quickly that Coach put a hand on the dash to steady himself.

"Damn, kid. Where's the fire?"

Dane turned onto the main road and accelerated toward town. It was a good thing he knew the route to the airport so well, because his mind was practically shutting down with disbelief.

This was bad. Impossibly bad. He didn't have a clue what to do about it.

And it was entirely his fault.

Fourteen

WILLOW LAY ON her sofa, staring up at the beams overhead. It was impressively quiet, except for the sounds an old house makes when it settles in for the night. She'd had twenty-four hours to process her awful conversation with Dane. But instead of feeling better, she had only become more depressed.

She sat up and reached for the phone, dialing Callie at home.

"Willow! How are you doing? I've been thinking about you all week."

She sighed. "Callie, I told him. And it could not have gone worse."

"Oh no," her friend sighed. "What did he say?"

"I..." Willow realized she didn't want to repeat it aloud. She didn't want to revisit his cruelty, it was just so mortifying, to have put herself in that position. "He was cold, Callie. Not a shred of empathy."

"Bastard!" Callie yelped.

"I wasn't expecting much—I told you that before. But it was truly awful. And now I'm embarrassed. Because I liked this guy—I really did..." her voice broke.

"Oh, sweetie. I'm so sorry."

"I thought I was a good judge of character," she cried. "I think I had this silly idea..." she couldn't even finish the sentence. But it was true. A tiny little part of Willow's heart had hoped that he would come around. She'd had no reason to think that he would—only the peculiar notion that he'd been as affected by her as she had by him.

It was ridiculous. And he'd turned out to be rotten.

Callie began to sound teary, too. "Honesty is supposed to be the best policy. But sometimes honesty bites us in the ass."

"He made it very clear that he expects me to terminate."

"Oh, my God. He *expects* you to? Isn't that your decision?"

"Of *course* it's my decision. But hearing him…ouch. It's harder to make my own decision now that I know how he really feels. I wish I could un-know it. I wish I could un-hear him say those words to me. He was scary, Callie. His face just died when I told him."

"Wait—scary how? Did he threaten you?"

Willow wiped her face with her sleeve. "No. Not at all. It's hard to explain, now that I think about it." She shivered, picturing the change on his face—eyes going from lit and intelligent to flat and dead. The place he'd gone inside his head…it was somewhere primal.

"You know what bothers me about that?" Callie asked. "Travis. Remember how he said the family was nuts? People say that all the time. But you think he meant it literally?"

"That sounds too Victorian, Callie. Like a chapter from *Wuthering Heights*. Mental illness isn't like hair color—jumping neatly from one kid to the next."

"You're the shrink."

"I'm the shrink who doesn't know what to think. I'm a bad Dr. Seuss rhyme."

"Willow, you have to hang in there, okay? This is the low point. You're going to take some very deep breaths.

And when you're good and ready, you'll make your decision."

"The hardest part?" Willow swallowed. "One of the things he said feels true."

Callie sighed. "I'll bet it isn't."

"He said, 'You really are a fuckup.' And it's hard to argue the point."

"No, it isn't," Callie argued. "Deep breaths, Willow. I mean it."

"Callie, a lot of things have gone wrong for me this year. But every one of them could be at least partially explained away by bad luck. But this one is all on me."

"Semantics. There were two people in that...Jeep."

"Bed, actually. Round two was when he said 'we don't have another condom' and I said 'it doesn't matter.'" Willow blew out a breath. Saying it out loud was bracing. "Only it *did* matter." She began crying again.

"Oh, Willow," Callie said again.

* * *

Dane had a splitting headache all the way across the Atlantic. A day later, he still suffered from it during the course inspection.

"And now we discover the pitfalls of training at low altitudes," Coach said, handing Dane another bottle of Evian water.

"Don't," Dane said, taking a swig. "I don't need you piling on me, too."

"Who's piling on you?" Coach asked. "I'm on your side, here. Let's get a better look at the fourth pitch," Coach suggested, sidestepping downhill. "I like the left side of the big jump." He put his thumbs together, palms out, as if framing a photograph. "That sets you up on the fall line into the carousel turn."

"Right." Dane rolled his head to the left and shook out his neck. He had to get his head in the game. Dane watched the competitors around him, leaning forward on their ski poles, moving their arms in a hypnotic way, like jellyfish tentacles, as they visualized hightailing it down the course. This was a Super-G course, meaning that the gates were few and far between, and speed rather than agility would win the day.

The usual race day mayhem surrounded them. Dane was never thrown off by the hundreds of people lined up just beyond the orange safety netting. He was never thrown off by competitors determined to beat him. And he was never thrown off by fear.

But today he was just plain thrown.

"Dane, are you going to be okay?" Coach asked for the hundredth time.

"Stop fucking asking me," he growled.

The truth was he was far from okay. Willow's announcement had rattled him to the core. Dane absolutely could *not* have a child. If he did, that meant that some poor kid would grow up just like him—waiting in dread for the symptoms to show up and tear his body apart. Watching the rest of the world get on with their lives.

And Willow would have to watch it all happen. She'd outlive her child by a good twenty years at least.

It wasn't supposed to happen this way. When Dane died, the family illness would stop killing people. He meant to be its very last victim.

He didn't sleep last night—he couldn't stop thinking about Willow. Her announcement had put him in the perverse position of hoping that she really *had* been sleeping around. It would be better for everyone if she was pregnant by someone else and only hoping to pin it on him. He tried to imagine that it was possible—that she'd done the math—figuring he'd made millions in endorsement money after the last Olympics.

Christ. She wasn't the type. She would never be the type.

Her unluckiest day was the day she'd met him.

Dane's headache had only partly receded by the time he made it into the start house. He was starting tenth, and the first seven were already down. There had been only one crash so far—an unlucky Norwegian who'd caught an edge on the second pitch, flying ass first into the safety netting. Dane bounced up and down in his ski boots to keep his feet warm.

"Danger."

He turned around to find one of his so-called teammates, a guy named J.P., calling to him. J.P. had scored a twelfth place start, better than he usually got.

"Yeah?" Why would the guy want to chitchat when he was three minutes from launch?

"I just heard the Germans radio up that the second jump is chewed on the left," J.P. said.

Dane stared him down. "Are you sure that's what they said?"

"*Ja. Absolut.* My mother is German." J.P. winked.

Dane flexed his knees, trying to think. He turned back to J.P. "Why isn't Harvey calling it up?"

J.P. shrugged. "No clue. But I'm taking the right side. Makes a nastier radius into the carousel, but if it keeps me on my feet...."

Fuck. Was this guy pulling his chain? Dane had already plotted his course. This asshole was probably just trying to rattle him. J.P. had never beat Dane in a race. But this year, the younger man was performing better than ever. Perhaps feeding a few doubts to Dane was part of his big strategy.

Dane heard his name called by the judge in the start house. He stepped forward, and his long boards were slammed onto the snow in front of him. Dane clipped in, staring down the course, clenching his jaw.

Coach hustled over, checking Dane's bindings. "What's the matter?" he asked quickly.

"Nothing. Fuck it," Dane said, snapping his goggles down. He shook out his quads, gripped the starting gate and stared on to the course. He focused his gaze right between the blue lines, while the start counter began to beep its warning pitch.

Behind him, his competitors began to call out. "Kill it, Dane! Like a boss!"

When the start counter chimed, he launched himself forward, poling madly to accelerate. Then gravity kicked in, the icy pitch slanting away beneath him until he felt the familiar roller-coaster drop. Dane tucked his poles under and bore down into an aerodynamic bullet position. The first turn was to the left. He rolled his skis onto their edges, his legs and boards hugging the slope, his muscles stepping up to handle the g-force of the sudden curve.

His headache forgotten, years of training and muscle memory kicked in. The next two turns came in quick succession, and he held his line. He was entering the fastest part of the course now. A lesser skier would lose his nerve, dialing back to keep things in check. But Dane watched the first jump rush up at him. He leaned his shoulders forward and welcomed the air. Over the years, dozens of journalists had used the phrase "death wish" to describe his aggressive style. In Dane's world, there were only two certainties—death and gravity. Every other human being on the planet lived with the same constraints, of course. It was just that Dane was more keenly aware of them than most other people ever were.

Dying in a high-speed crash would be no worse than wasting away in a nursing home. Any risk was justifiable when no one depended on you. Who would it even hurt?

Willow.

Even as he reached seventy-five miles an hour, the image of her shot through his guilty brain. And even that infinitesimally brief flicker of her was enough to alter his consciousness. As he landed the first jump, his skis hit the snow at almost the same nanosecond. Almost, but not quite. There was a bobble in his right ski. He squared his shoulders and corrected his position, preparing for a hard turn to the right.

Unfortunately, he overcorrected. And now, even bearing down like a tank at the next turn, he swung it wide. That's how things always unraveled—one misaligned turn led to an even bigger one. Each mistake raised the stakes for the next one, leading to even bigger corrections.

Just like real life.

He was about four feet further to skiers' left than he'd planned to be when the second jump came into view. And just like J.P. had said, it was chewed all to hell. But it was far too late to change course. All he could do was watch the lip come for him, the ice yanking his skis apart as he launched.

Flung clumsily into the air, his weight too far back on his hips, Dane windmilled his arms to try for a better position. But the universe wasn't having it. He landed one ski perfectly. And the other one caught a sickening edge as it came down off-kilter, snapping the ski from the binding at the first pressure he put on it.

And then came the inevitable terror of flying down the hill in little more than a body stocking, nothing but goggles and a helmet to protect himself. He edged his remaining ski as best he could, dumping maybe twenty miles per hour before it, too, gave out under pressure. His body flew on past, flinging Dane chest first into the netting.

It might have been okay, if he'd landed facing the sky. But the full two hundred pounds of him landed on his right knee. There was no telltale pop of ligaments separating. Only a sudden pain, and then a strange snowy numbness in his leg.

The first person to reach him was a gate judge. "*Va tutto bene?*" the man asked. *Are you all right?*

Hell no. He was not.

* * *

He must have blacked out, because the next thing he noticed was a man shining a light in his eyes while yammering away in Italian. He was strapped down to something. The sled? He raised his head. He was on a stretcher at the bottom of the hill. There seemed to be a hundred people standing around.

Must be bad. "Coach?"

"Kid," it was Coach's voice. "You got your bell rung."

Dane stared up at Coach, but unfortunately there were two of him. "That all?"

"Not sure," Coach hedged. "You told them the pain in your right leg was a nine."

Christ.

"Danger, dude. I'm so sorry." It was a new voice.

Dane looked up to find a blurry version of J.P. standing over him. "The fuck you are," Dane muttered. "This works in your favor."

"*Jesus*, dude. That's harsh." Both J.P.s were shaking their heads. "Hang in there."

There was another burst of Italian chatter and Dane felt himself lifted. His body was jostled in the air. A shot of fire ripped down his leg. Dane gasped and closed his eyes.

Fifteen

WILLOW'S PHONE BUZZED while she was at work. Callie's text read: *Did you read the sports page today?*

Willow, who never read the sports page, replied: *Why?*

Callie's answer was: *Read it. And then call me.*

The headline made Willow gasp. "Olympian Danger Hollister's Season Ends Early With Broken Knee In Italy."

She dialed Callie at home. "It's going to sound vain, but I feel responsible," she said.

"Willow, it can only be your fault if you flew to Italy and pushed him off the hill. Which would not have been a bad plan."

"You always snap me out of it, Callie." Still, his brother died, and now his leg was broken. And she'd told him she was pregnant, all in the same week.

"Well, guess who is flying in for surgery tonight? They're putting two screws into his tibia. The way the entire ortho unit is running around, you'd think the queen was coming to dine."

"No way! Do you think you'll be assigned to him?" Callie worked as an inpatient hospitalist at the Windsor County Medical Center.

"I hope not. In fact, no way. If Asshole Baby Daddy's file falls in my hands I'll swap him for another patient."

Willow laughed. "That's very loyal of you. But you don't have to do that."

"Seriously. It would be just too tempting to forget to order his pain meds."

"You always make me smile."

* * *

A day later Willow got one more text: *Asshole assigned to my asshole ex.*

To which she replied: *How fitting.*

Willow did her best not to think about Dane after that. What she really needed to do was distance herself from him and figure out her own life. Telling him had been a real error. She couldn't stop hearing him say, *you really are a fuckup.* And feeling like one was not a good frame of mind, not for someone who needed to make a big decision.

So Willow went to yoga class, and in Child's Pose tried to open her heart to the possibilities. She'd begun reading adoption websites in her spare time. There were many families standing ready to adopt. Willow knew this. But she had grown up knowing that her parents didn't love her enough to keep her, and she had vowed many times over never to do that to a child.

And now here she was, considering that very thing.

Willow put her forehead on the yoga mat and tried to center her flailing soul. The decision would not be rushed.

* * *

But even breathing exercises could not prepare her for the shock of seeing a certain green Jeep climb her driveway two days later. At the kitchen window, she froze as the driver's side door opened. Coach stepped out, and she heaved a sigh of relief. But of course it was Coach. Men with broken legs did not drive Jeeps.

Willow had turned back to the shopping list she was working on when she heard raised voices.

"I can't stay here."

Willow's neck prickled with recognition. She peeked out the kitchen window.

"Get out of the fucking Jeep, Dane!" Coach had opened the tailgate and was addressing someone in the back. "I'm not carrying you up your flight of stairs on Main Street just because you're a stubborn son of a bitch."

Whatever Dane said next, Willow didn't hear it. But Coach leaned a set of crutches against the tailgate and then stormed off toward the apartment. And then absolutely nothing at all happened for a few minutes. When Dane's coach reappeared, Willow made herself back away from the window. She stared, sightlessly, at her shopping list until low voices receded slowly past her door. Then she hopped back over to the window for one glimpse of Dane leaning heavily on his coach, hopping slowly along on one foot toward the apartment. His head was down, his shoulders bent.

He looked beaten.

Sixteen

TWO MORE DAYS passed before Willow saw either Dane or Coach. She worked extra hours at the insurance agency, and she met Callie for yoga. The pregnancy began to announce itself in a few subtle ways. She was suddenly exhausted all the time, falling into bed at nine o'clock and sleeping like the dead.

Then one morning, as Willow was just about to climb into her truck to go to work, Coach had come outside to speak to her.

"Morning," she said, her keys in her hand.

"Good morning," he echoed, an apologetic look on his face. "I was hoping I could ask you a little favor."

"Sure," she said, shifting from foot to foot. "I should have already asked if you two had everything you need."

"I've got him on the pull-out sofa," Coach said. "It's fine. But today I'm supposed to drive up to the Burke Mountain School for a meeting. Would you mind just putting your head in this afternoon, asking him if he needs anything? I never did get around to getting a landline put in," he said. "But I think I should."

Willow swallowed. "Sure. I can do that."

"He looks a little out of it this morning. I just worry that he'll fall or something. Shit. Don't tell him I said that."

"Um, okay," Willow had agreed. "If you need me to."

"I'd feel better if somebody checked on him. And I'm sure he'll be happy to see a face that isn't mine."

Don't bet on it, Willow thought. At least it settled one question she'd had on her mind—Coach clearly had no clue about her pregnancy and Dane's harsh opinion of it. "It would be my pleasure," she lied.

* * *

A couple of hours later, Willow found herself tapping lightly on the apartment's door. When nobody answered, she knocked again.

She heard only silence from inside. Given their recent fiery conversation, she knew full well that he wouldn't want anything to do with her. But what if he *had* fallen down?

Willow turned the knob and pushed the door open. She was startled to see Dane's eyes trained on her from where he lay on the pull-out couch. His expression was unreadable. She stepped all the way in and closed the door behind her. "Hi," she said with caution. The way he stared at her was unnerving. "Coach asked me to make sure you have everything you need."

He closed his eyes for a second, and then opened them. Today they were the color of a stormy sea. "You're not real," he said, his voice hoarse.

The hair stood up on the back of Willow's neck. "Sorry?"

He swallowed thickly. "You're not here," he said.

"Dane?" she took a couple of steps closer. His lips looked unnaturally dry and there were beads of sweat on his forehead. Tentatively, she reached down and put her hand on his brow. "Oh, my God." He was burning up.

His big arm came up off the bed then, clamping down on her hand, pinning her hand to his head. "Not supposed to do this," he said.

"Do what?" she whispered, her mind reeling. She had to call someone. His fever must be off the charts.

"Touch her," he said. "Not allowed." He folded his big hand over hers and held on.

"Dane," she whispered, her heart racing. Willow slipped her hand out from under his. "I have to make a phone call," she said.

But Dane wasn't having it. With surprising speed, he grabbed her other hand instead. "No." His fingers around hers were hot and dry. His blue eyes stared up at her, vulnerable.

"Dane," she said firmly. "Let me make the call, and I'll come back."

In answer, he only held on tighter. She could probably just wrench her hand away, but she was afraid of his reaction. If he got upset and began flailing around, what would happen? Would a feverish person be mindful of his own broken knee?

She would try reverse psychology. Willow sat on the edge of the bed and put her free hand onto his, which gripped her. "I'm not going anywhere."

He squeezed her hands as his eyes fluttered closed. Willow waited a minute or so, wondering how she'd gotten herself involved. She would call Coach first. If he didn't answer, she'd call Callie. Dane's eyes didn't open again, so Willow counted to ten and then tried to slip her hands out of his.

"No," he said, holding on, his eyes still shut.

Willow sighed. She looked down at his big hand wrapped around hers. In her dreams, he came to her, these hands reaching out to hold her, to apologize. But the only version of Dane who wanted her nearby was the one rendered temporarily insane by fever. "Dane," she tried. "I thought you weren't supposed to touch me."

His eyes flew open and then fluttered closed again. "Not real," he said with a sigh. "S'okay."

"Good to know." Willow listened to the old clock on the wall tick and wondered what she should do.

"Can't have you," he whispered. His face creased with pain. "Not ever."

Her neck prickled again. "Why?" she whispered. Or maybe she just thought the word. And maybe he didn't even know what he was saying.

Why did everything have to be such a tangled mess?

Willow watched his face. His jaw relaxed, his forehead became smooth. With his face peaceful, he reminded her of a Renaissance painting—all masculine lines and draped fabric. His chest rose and fell under the sheet. After a few more minutes, his grasp on her hand went slack. She slipped away, tiptoed for the door and ran back to her house.

* * *

Coach did not answer his phone, which was hardly surprising. She had only a vague idea of where Burke was, but she knew it was in northern Vermont, where the mobile phone coverage was even spottier than it was here.

Tracking Callie down was something that often took time. So Willow called the main hospital number and asked them to page her. "Is this an emergency?" the receptionist asked.

"As a matter of fact, it is."

Willow's phone rang a few minutes later. "What's the matter?" Callie asked, breathless. "Are you okay?"

"I'm fine," Willow said. "But Dane has a high fever."

"How high?"

"No idea," Willow sighed. "But Coach asked me to check on him, and his forehead is like a radiator. Also, he says I'm not real."

"Crap," Callie said. "Postsurgical infections can be nasty. I don't suppose you looked at the incision?"

"No," Willow said. "I called you instead."

There was a silence while her friend thought it through. "Of course you can't move him. He can't crutch out to the car like that, if he's insensible and thinks you're his dead aunt Zelda."

"Trust me, he's not getting up to go anywhere."

"I think you have to call 9-1-1, Willow. If he has a staph infection, it could kill him. If your gut says his fever is high…"

"It is. I always thought 'burning up with fever' was a cliché. I don't anymore."

"Okay. Then put him on a bus and send him our way."

* * *

Willow called 9-1-1 and asked them to send an ambulance. Then she left a message for Coach. Finally, she carried her cordless phone back to the apartment, having no idea whether or not it would work back there. When she opened the door, Dane's eyes were still closed, but he was trembling.

She went into the little bathroom and wet the hand towel with cold water. After wringing it out, she placed it over his forehead.

"Christ," he said suddenly.

"Sorry," she whispered.

His hands were shaking with fever, and it frightened her. She picked both of them up just to make it stop. Willow held his hands in her lap and watched the clock.

It took fifteen minutes until she heard tires in the driveway, and Willow reminded herself never to have a heart attack in rural Vermont. She ran to the door, waving to the two EMTs who would otherwise have knocked on her kitchen door.

"I'm Bill," the first EMT said. "How are we doing?" He was a guy about Willow's age. His partner was a woman with a Mohawk and a piercing through the middle of her nose.

"Well," Willow began, "my friend here had knee surgery at the hospital a few days ago. And now I think he has a high fever. I called the hospital, and the doctor is worried about an infection. I'd drive him in but..." she opened the door.

"...but he's an enormous motherfucker," Bill said, striding over to the bed.

"Language," warned the woman.

Bill tapped Dane gently on the hand. "I'm Bill," he said. Dane didn't move. Bill put his wrist on Dane's cheek. "Winner. That's a big fever all right." He held Dane's wrist, clocking his pulse.

"So I'm not crazy?" Willow asked.

"Not about that," Bill agreed. "Besides the surgery, any other medical issues?"

"I wouldn't know," Willow answered.

"We'll get the stretcher."

* * *

Willow got out of the way when they wheeled the stretcher inside. "His right knee is broken," she said.

"We'll take care," the woman said. "Let's have a look." She peeled the sheets off a Dane.

His eyes flew open. "Finn?"

"I'm Rhonda," she said. "I'm just going to take a look at your knee. You're going to be fine."

"Finn?" he asked again, his voice panicky. Willow's heart splintered at the sound of his plea for his brother. She did not know what to say. "Coach?" Dane tried.

"He's on his way," Willow said. "You'll see him soon."

He craned his neck at the sound of her voice. His eyes were frighteningly unfocused.

Bill had maneuvered a board underneath Dane. "On three," he said. "One, two…" He and Rhonda lifted ends of the board, transferring Dane to the stretcher. Moving quickly, Bill clicked straps across Dane's chest and hips.

Dane didn't like it. He tried lifting his head off the stretcher.

"Easy," Bill said. "This is just for the ride."

But Dane was having none of it. He shook his torso from side to side, and the stretcher rocked.

"Hey now," Rhonda warned. She flicked a glance at Willow. "A little help here?"

Willow stepped up to the stretcher and looked down at him. "Dane," she said. His eyes swam onto her. "You're a little sick, and you have to see a doctor."

"Not the nursing home," he said.

"Nursing home?" Willow shook her head. "Of course not. And Coach will meet you at the...doctor's."

Dane's hand flapped. It was held in by his side by a strap at his wrist. He was trying to reach for her. So Willow took his hand. "You feel good," he said.

"We can't allow you to ride in the bus," Rhonda said. "But you can follow us."

Willow considered this idea. She could easily climb into her truck and follow them. But Dane, when conscious, didn't want a thing to do with her. And because she wasn't family, the hospital would make her wait in the waiting room. If she went, it would mean sitting on a plastic chair all night, for someone who did not love her and never would.

The awful thing was, she was quite willing to do it.

That's really pathetic, she told herself. Even as Dane tightened his grip on her hand, she knew what she had to do. She would let that ambulance roll down her driveway, and then she would go back inside the house and stay there. It was for the best.

* * *

Dane held tight to the angel's hand, even as the bed began to move. She tried to let go, but he held on tight.

"No," he said.

"Can't fit you *and* her through the door, sport," said a voice. A pair of hands separated his from the angel's, and he didn't like it. So he let them know. By yelling. But the bed beneath him moved anyway. He yelled louder.

"Jesus, hold his fucking hand already," the voice said. The angel's hand slipped back into his.

The air was now colder, which felt good on his face. There was winter light, which made everything better. But the ride was bumpier, and he felt spears of pain in his knee. "Fuck," he said. The angel's hand squeezed his.

"Almost there," the voice promised. Then he felt himself being lifted. "Shoulda had my Wheaties cereal this morning," the voice complained.

He lost the angel's hand.

Christ.

Seventeen

IT WASN'T REALLY lunchtime yet, but Willow had ducked away from her desk at the insurance agency. Shrugging on her coat, her plan was to grab a bagel from the little market on the corner. It had been such an awful, nauseated morning. She had already thrown up once in the agency bathroom, flushing the toilet to cover the sound of her retching. She hadn't got the hang of morning sickness yet. But carbs seemed to help tame the dragon in her gut.

Also, the cool outdoor air seemed to help. So Willow took her time walking toward the deli, peeking into the windows of the ski shops that lined the street. There was a delivery truck pulled up next to Rupert's Bar and Grill. A metal conveyor slide stretched onto the sidewalk, and one burly guy in a knit cap hustled cases of beer down the ramp, while another grabbed them off, stacking them onto a hand truck.

Willow paused, considering her options for navigating around them. But even as she did so, the smell of stale beer mixed with the urine that some late-night customer had aimed into the gutter stabbed her nostrils. All at once, Willow felt the telltale signs of another bout of morning sickness—too much saliva in her mouth, the rising panic in her throat.

Her path blocked, Willow veered into the door of Rupert's, which was propped open for the delivery. Inside, she ran straight past a startled Travis and into the empty ladies' room. There, she leaned over the toilet and gagged violently. Her body managed to throw up only a pathetic amount of…she didn't like to think what. But at least she would feel slightly better now.

Willow took her time wiping her mouth, flushing away the evidence and then washing her hands. She rinsed her mouth repeatedly, blinked her watering eyes and checked her reflection in the mirror. It was startling to see that the Willow looking back looked almost normal. Sure, there was a pallor there, but it was late January. And her eyes were a bit red. But given the way she felt inside, she ought to have seen a many-headed mythological beast looking back in the mirror. It was time to sneak out of here and get back to work.

"Willow, are you okay?" Travis was waiting for her right outside the door, a concerned expression on his face. *Damn.*

She stood up a little straighter, throwing her shoulders back. "Sure, Travis, I'm fine. Just a little…" She cleared her throat. "Emergency. Sorry."

He folded his arms, leaning against the wall. "You sure? You look pale."

"Sure, I'm sure." If only it were true. She could still feel her mouth watering uncomfortably. What she needed was to get away from here and buy a bagel. That would settle everything down. She would have never believed that eating food could cure nausea. But morning sickness was a different beast than any other stomach upset she'd ever experienced.

"Okay," he said, still watching her. "I've been thinking about you."

That got her attention. Willow's eyes snapped to his, and what she found there was startling. Her friend's green eyes were soft, like an open question. The corners of his mouth tugged upward in a handsome smile.

"Would you have dinner with me, Willow?"

She hesitated. "I don't know, Travis, I'm kind of..." she swallowed. Her empty stomach turned over on itself, and she steeled herself against the sensation. If she didn't do something soon, she'd be dry heaving in the ladies' room again shortly. "Travis, I..." she put a hand to her mouth, trying to get control.

His expression changed to a quizzical one, and then flickered with trouble. "Come with me, Willow," he said, turning around. He walked straight towards an open doorway.

Willow drew in the deepest breath she could muster and followed him. By the time she walked into the big commercial kitchen, Travis had already grabbed something out of an open crock by the soup station. He cracked the cellophane on a little packet and held it out to her on his palm.

She took the packet of saltines, broke one and popped it into her mouth before the surprise set in. And then Willow felt her face begin to redden. She ate the other half of the cracker and began to feel a little steadier. She looked up into Travis's eyes again, not knowing what she'd find there. It was bad enough that she had yet to make the decision of a lifetime. But now all her troubles were laid bare for him to see.

But when she met his gaze, it was steady. "I guess my timing is pretty horrible, right? Trying to ask you out on a date while you're trying not to puke."

"How did you know?" she asked.

He leaned back against the stainless-steel prep counter. "I pay attention to you, Willow." His eyes dipped to the floor for a moment, but then they came back steady. "Also, I've seen it before. It was pretty soon after my girlfriend started throwing up every morning that I ended up married to a woman who didn't love me. Hopefully that won't happen to you."

Willow's eyes felt hot. Whenever she thought of the terrible conversation she'd had with Dane about her pregnancy, her face burned with shame, as if she'd actually done what he'd accused her of doing. It didn't make any sense at all. But the sting of his rejection was fierce. "I wouldn't worry about that," she told Travis, her voice unsteady. "Marriage is really low on the list of probable outcomes," she said, attempting a smile.

Travis blew out a breath. "You don't sound at all happy. If it's anyone I know…if someone's being a jerk about it…I'm happy to try to talk some sense into him."

She shook her head. "I'm not ready. I can't talk about it. Because I don't know what I'm going to do."

"Okay," he said slowly. "I won't say another word. No—that's not true. I have to say one more thing, and it's this: it can happen to *anyone*. You know that, right?" His green eyes searched her face.

Willow nodded, but her eyes filled with tears anyway. Because that truth was that she wasn't at all sure that it could happen to anyone. It seemed like something that only happened to fuckups like her.

"Aw, Willow," Travis sighed. "And we *are* going to have dinner. If only because you look like you could really use a friend." He stepped forward to wrap his arms around her. "I'm sorry for your troubles."

She returned the hug. "I appreciate it. I really do. You have no idea."

Eighteen

THE PHONE COMPANY truck spent all morning in Willow's driveway. Following Dane's infection scare, it seemed Coach wasn't taking any more chances. After the truck finally departed, another one rolled up the gravel, this one from UPS.

Willow signed for a box addressed to Dane. But then she hesitated. There was no green Jeep in the driveway, which meant that Coach wasn't home. Willow stood there in the driveway, considering her options. She couldn't leave the box in the snow; that would be rude. The shipping label was from a medical facility in New Hampshire, so there was every likelihood that Willow was holding Dane's brother's personal effects.

With a sigh, she walked up to the door. Maybe Coach and Dane had left together for a doctor's appointment? She could just slip the box inside the door.

* * *

Unfortunately, Dane was napping when Willow came in. The sound of the door opening stirred him from a pleasant dream. So for the first few seconds after he opened his eyes, he didn't remember the ugly truth. All he saw was her pretty face, her graceful shape as she closed the door of the apartment against the cold. He might even have begun to smile.

But when she turned her face toward him, there was fear on it. And then he was awake, and arranging his own expression into an unrevealing mask.

"Hi," she said cautiously. "This just came for you."

He saw her hesitate with the box, wondering where to put it. She looked like she was on the verge of dropping it and running for the door. So he blurted out his question. "Willow, did you have an abortion?"

Her mouth fell open. "You did *not* just ask me that."

Dane swallowed. "I'm not trying to torture you, I just need to know."

Standing in front of him, she took a deep, shaky breath. "I'm not discussing it with you."

"That's a mistake," he said quietly. "Anyone who has a child of mine will live to regret it."

He watched her inhale carefully. "You made that point already," she said. "And even so, I honestly believed that after the shock wore off, you'd be more civilized. But since that's not possible. I'm leaving now."

It gutted him. Willow stood before him, shaking with unhappiness. And yet she never backed down. A lesser woman would throw the first heavy object she could find right at his head. But she just stared him down, vulnerable but real.

It was all he could do to keep from reaching for her as she put the box down a few feet away from him. Then she turned toward the door.

"Wait." His voice was thick. "You said your friend is a doctor. What's her specialty?"

Willow's eyes darted around to his face, disbelief shining in them. "Internal medicine."

"Can I have her number, please?"

"God, *why*?"

"I'm not sure I have the right specialist, and I want her opinion."

Willow sucked in air. He could see her trying to hold herself together. It hurt to watch. It hurt to have her so close and hating him. She scraped her phone from her pocket and looked up the number. With shaking hands she jotted it down on the edge of the newspaper on the coffee table. Then she threw it on his chest. "Her name is Callie Anders," she said. "But I doubt she'll talk to you."

Willow stormed out and slammed the door.

Dane listened to the sound of her footsteps retreating. Then he took the brand-new phone in his hand. He'd managed to put this off his entire adult life. But no more.

He dialed Callie's office, but of course, she didn't answer. A perky receptionist took the call. And when he asked for Callie, he was told she was with a patient. "Would you like to leave a message?"

"I would," he said. "My name is Dane, and I'm calling with regard to Willow Reade. Dr. Anders will want to speak with me. It's urgent."

* * *

Ten minutes later the phone rang. "Hello, this is Dane," he answered.

"This is Callie Anders." Her voice was curt. "You left me a message. About Willow?"

He cleared his throat. "Callie, I asked Willow for your number. I suppose you know who I am?"

She hesitated. "Yes."

"I need to ask for a favor," he said slowly. "But it's really a favor for Willow."

"What, then?" her voice was strained.

"First of all," he said, "it's highly confidential."

She sighed. "Go on."

"Could you…" she was not going to like this one bit. "I'd come to your office, but I can't drive…"

"…I heard."

"Okay. I would like you to come out here, preferably when Willow's not around. I need you to draw my blood. You won't need more than a couple of vials."

There was a loaded silence on her end while the good doctor did the math. She would know that there was only one reason he'd ask her to draw blood. To test him for a disease—a disease that she would now assume could infect Willow. "Dane, I don't know who you think you are, but you're scaring the shit out of me right now."

"And I wouldn't be doing that," he kept his voice level. "If it wasn't important."

She paused again. "What am I testing you for?"

"I'll tell you when you come."

She whistled. "You really are an asshole."

"Yes, doctor, I am."

There was another long silence, and he thought she might hang up. "There's a yoga class that Willow goes to at seven. I'll come then." She hung up on him.

* * *

Willow fed chips of beeswax into the wide-open mouth of the jar, where the gorgeous yellow substance melted into a pretty swirl. She turned the saucepan of water down to a simmer and used an old knife to cut through yet another old candle stub. Her kitchen was perfumed with the honeyed smell of melting wax.

Even as she worked—melting down old candle stubs into precious beeswax—she could feel Dane's presence. As much as she tried to forget about him, he was like a hum in her head. When she sat reading on her sofa or stood scrubbing out a pot at her sink, he was mere yards away. The Dane who had wormed his way into her heart had bright eyes and an easy laugh. That one had clung to her, as if he never wanted to let her go. *What you do to me*, he'd sighed.

She wished she could stop thinking about that man. Because the one around back in the apartment was the one whose eyes darkened at the sight of her and who said ugly things meant to hurt her. That man was afraid of something, and she didn't know what. Willow wished she could stop thinking about him. She had her own needs to consider and a big decision to make. But it needled at her. If she knew why he was so angry, maybe she'd be better able to identify her own feelings under the jumble of wreckage in her heart.

Or maybe that was just a cop out.

The decision was plenty difficult even without Dane's acidic disapproval. Willow wanted a baby. That part was easy. But she never thought she'd do it alone. Yet waiting around for the right partner didn't seem to be working. They would be a tiny family of two. It wouldn't be easy, but nothing good ever was.

Willow turned off the stove's heat and stirred her candle wax with a chopstick.

There was only one hurdle she really couldn't see how to get over. Someday, the baby would ask her. "Who is my father?"

And Willow feared the only answer she could give the child would be: "a man who won't even look at us." It just didn't seem fair. Willow herself had grown up knowing that her parents didn't want her enough to keep her. And now she would inflict at least a portion of that same doubt on her child, from the moment of his or her birth.

Which decision was more selfish? To keep the baby, knowing it would be shadowed by its father's animosity forever? Or to take another way out, and never have to try to explain?

She just didn't know.

* * *

Dane heard the gravel under Willow's wheels just after six thirty. By seven, Coach was sitting on the end of his bed, and they were watching a boxing match. The knock came a few minutes later.

"Are you expecting anyone?" Coach asked, getting up to answer it.

"Actually I am."

Coach's eyebrows went up, and he opened the door. "Hello, there!"

Dane recognized Callie from that night at the bar. Her eyes flickered between Coach and Dane. "Hi, I'm Willow's friend Callie."

"Nice to meet you, Callie!" Coach said. "Can I get you a drink?"

She shook her head.

"Coach," Dane said. "I'm sorry, but could you give us ten minutes?"

His face fell. "Sure, kid. I'm going to run out for beer." He shrugged his jacket on and went outside, closing the door behind him.

Callie carried a small blue cooler with her. He knew she would show up and do this thing for him, because he'd really left her no other choice. She sat down on a wooden dining chair. "I brought the stuff, but first you have to tell me what this is about." Her eyes were wide and questioning.

"Did Willow have an abortion?" he asked.

Callie's jaw dropped. "I'm not going to tell you that. You dragged me out here for that? To invade her privacy?"

Dane pointed at her cooler. "I'm just trying to figure out if we need that."

The doctor's face creased with confusion. "Well, don't we? If you're infected with…"

"With what, Callie? I'm sure you came up with a few theories on the trip over here. Let's hear them."

She blinked. "I won't play games with you. You tell me *right now* what the danger is, or I'm leaving."

Dane swallowed, reading on her face that she meant it. The trouble was that Dane had never said it aloud. Never. Not once. *I probably have…* The words stuck in his throat as she stared at him.

"Enough." She stood up.

He coughed once. "My mother died from Huntington's disease." He watched her face.

Callie sucked in her breath and dropped back onto the chair. Slowly, her eyes filled with tears.

Dane chuckled. "That's what everyone says. Everyone who's been to medical school." He shifted in the bed. "You were thinking HIV, right? That would have been a bummer, but controllable with drugs." He rolled up the sleeve of his flannel shirt. "Or maybe you thought about hepatitis C. Now there's a nasty disease. But look on the bright side, Dr. Callie. Even if you're clumsy with that needle, you can't catch what I've got. And neither did Willow, obviously."

"But the *baby* might have it," Callie whispered, wiping her tears away with the palms of her hands. "And you've never had the genetic test? And now you have to. For Willow."

He looked up at the ceiling. "If she already had an abortion, then I don't need it at all." He waited.

She gaped at him. "You're putting me in an impossible situation."

"Really? Would you like to trade places with me?" She didn't say anything, so he continued. "When I was a kid, waiting outside my mother's hospital room, this whole crowd of medical students files out. The attending brought them all in to see the Huntington's patient. Because they'd probably never see another one again, right? Too weird, too rare. So one of these students says to his friend, '*That's* the disease that makes me say, whatever happens to me, I'll be fine. Because I don't have to die of Huntington's.'"

He looked at Callie, but she just stared at him, fear in her face. And then, very slowly, she leaned over and picked up the cooler. "Willow hasn't..." she stopped herself. "I think you do need the test. Have you considered that knowing might be a relief?"

He couldn't take his eyes off her hands, which were unwrapping the sterile tube. His stomach knotted. "No way. I would *never* have done the test. But Willow's forcing me."

"This isn't Willow's fault."

"Yeah, it kind of is," he said as his hands began to sweat. *Liar. You broke your own rule.* He took in a shaky breath. "At least I got a little something out of it. Willow was a good lay."

The look on Callie's face could have been bottled and sold as repellent. "Here's a tip, Dane. Don't say things like that to a woman who's about to stab you." She snapped on a pair of latex gloves, and then ripped open an alcohol wipe.

He thrust his arm toward her. "I have a broken leg and a fatal disease. You couldn't hurt me with that thing worse than I hurt already." It should have sounded tough, but his throat caught on the words.

She scraped his arm with the disinfectant. "If my memory is correct, your odds of inheriting Huntington's are fifty percent," she said. "What if you're in the clear and a total asshole for nothing?"

Dane shook his head. "In my family, we don't do fifty percent," he explained.

She hooked the tube to the vial and uncapped the syringe. "You'll feel a—"

"*Do it,*" he cut her off. "I get blood drawn every fucking month for drug tests."

He felt the tug of his blood into the syringe, where it would flow through the tube and into the vial.

"Other people have troubles, too, you know," the doctor said softly.

"Cry me a river," he said.

She sighed. "I don't suppose you know that Willow lived in six different foster homes before she turned eighteen."

"No shit?" he whispered.

"No shit," the doctor answered. In the silence she changed vials.

"Well. I guess her bad luck hadn't run out yet, then," he said.

"I guess not," Callie said, her voice shaking with fury.

And then it was done. She put the vials on ice, and slapped a bandage on his arm. "What name am I putting on these?"

"Daffy Duck," he said. "If you put my own name on it, you might as well kill me right now."

She took two steps toward the door.

"I'll pay in cash," he said. "Just tell me where to send it."

She sighed and turned around. "You know, it can probably be tested in utero, too. Even if you are positive..."

"You won't be telling Willow. Doctor-patient privilege."

Her eyes were wet. "If it weren't for Willow, I would tell you to go right to hell."

Dane adjusted his pillow. "Everyone else does." He picked up the TV remote. "We need the results before the end of her first trimester," he said. "The abortion will be easier on her."

The door slammed shut after Callie went out.

Coach came back a few minutes later. "You okay?" he asked.

Dane turned the volume of the fight up. "Good as I ever was," he said over the noise.

Nineteen

ON A VERY cold night the following week, Willow made homemade gnocchi for dinner. She was still craving carbs. And her dinner guest—Callie—was a willing accomplice. She made a long-simmered sauce Bolognese as well.

"So, how goes it with your surly neighbor?" Callie asked.

Willow shook her head. "I've seen him once since his episode. And the only thing he wanted to talk about was your phone number. He wanted to ask you about specialists at the hospital. Did he call?"

Callie looked pained. "I didn't return the call."

"I told him you wouldn't." They ate in silence for a few minutes, but there was something weighing on Willow. "Callie," she asked. "I want to ask you something. But don't assume..." she trailed off.

"What is it, sweetie?"

Willow put down her fork. "I just want to make sure I've weighed every single option, okay? So I'm curious about what doctors think of abortion. How does medical school, well, inform your opinion about it?"

Her friend paled. "Willow...I thought you wanted..."

"I'm not sure what I want yet," her friend said. "I'm just curious, okay? After med school, are most doctors pro-choice?"

Callie looked caught. "Well...in med school you learn a lot about horrible birth defects, so..." Her friend drew in a deep breath.

"Callie?" Willow asked. "Are you okay?"

Her friend shook her head. "I just really can't talk about this right now," she said. "I'm so sorry."

She had never seen Callie tongue-tied before. Willow wondered if she had inadvertently asked her friend a question that was more personal than she would have guessed.

"Okay," Willow said quietly. "I've made a lot of irresponsible decisions the past few years. I'm trying on this idea, because I don't want to make any more of them."

"Willow, how many weeks are you?"

She watched Callie's face, which was curiously ashen. "I'm six weeks. Why?"

"You have more time to think about this, then," Callie said. "Take some more time."

"I will." Willow ate another bite. But Callie only pushed the food around on her plate. "Are you okay, Callie? You look really tired."

"I haven't been sleeping," her friend admitted. "It's been a really hard week."

"I'm sorry to hear that," Willow said. "Have a glass of wine? One of us should."

* * *

When Willow drove home from work the next Monday, she found herself following a green Jeep down the road, and then up her own driveway. They parked side by side, and Willow glanced into the vehicle, feeling great relief when she saw that Coach was in there alone.

"Hi, Coach," she said, getting out.

"Willow!" he said. "How are you?"

"Good," she said brightly, though it was a lie. Willow still doubted that Coach knew her scary little secret. And she sure as hell didn't want to involve him.

"Willow, I hate to ask…" he tilted his head to the side.

"Do you need something?"

He opened the trunk of his car with an exasperated sigh. "Is there a chance I could run a load of laundry through your machine? I had no idea that the Laundromat would be closed today." He pulled out a laundry bag and a bottle of detergent.

"Oh, sure!" she said. If only all of life's problems were so easily fixed. "Follow me."

* * *

"I really appreciate this," Coach said, emerging from Willow's laundry room, his bottle of detergent hooked over her thumb. "I'm a little overwhelmed taking care of Mr. Grumpy. There's nobody so miserable as a laid-up skier during racing season."

Willow did not want to land on the topic of Dane. "The wash cycle takes about forty-five minutes," she said. "If you play your cards right, you'll be a few minutes late. And just in time to eat one of these, hot out of the oven." She'd left a batch of bread dough rising on the counter top while she was away at work, and now she stood at the counter, shaping them into rolls.

"Well that is something to look forward to," he said. "In the meantime, I'll check on his lordship."

She couldn't help it. Willow laughed.

Coach winked at her on his way out the door.

* * *

When he tapped on the door again, Willow was just removing the first batch of rolls from the oven. "Come in," she called.

"Lordy, it smells good in here," Coach said.

"Toss your laundry in the dryer, and I'll butter one for you," she offered.

When he reappeared, she pushed a plate toward him, the roll steaming and butter oozing across the torn surface. "Coffee?" she asked.

"I don't want to be any trouble," he said.

She waved a hand. "I'm having one."

"I'd love one." Coach sat down on a stool and beamed at her. He had a very kind face, and the sort of demeanor that made it easy to feel comfortable in his presence.

Willow turned toward the espresso machine and began to tamp down a shot. She would make herself a tiny coffee with a lot of milk in it. It was strange, but lately she'd found herself behaving like a pregnant lady. She'd cut down her coffee consumption to almost nothing. And she didn't take anything for the headache she'd had over the weekend. Her mind might run in an endless loop of indecision, but she took good care of her pregnant body. Her subconscious clearly wanted in on the decision.

"So, what is it about Mondays in Vermont?" Coach asked, chewing. "Everything is closed. Driving up to the shuttered Laundromat felt like the last straw."

"Tell me about it," Willow smiled. "It's restaurants, too. It took me a while to figure that out after I moved here.

Don't get hungry on a Monday. I think it's because they cater to the tourists from Connecticut, so closing Sundays is a bad idea."

"Ah," Coach bit into his roll. "Wow," he said, chewing. "This is amazing."

"There's nothing like warm bread to lift your spirits," Willow agreed. And hers could really use a lift.

"So you're not a native Vermonter?" Coach asked.

Willow laughed. "Far from. I grew up in Philadelphia."

"You still have family there?" he asked.

It was an innocent enough question. He had no way of knowing how difficult the topic really was. "No family," she said, without elaborating. Technically, Willow couldn't be sure this was actually true. But after the state stepped in after neighbors had leveled charges of neglect, Willow had never seen her parents again. She had only the shakiest memory of their faces.

Coach was studying her. "Another member of the club, then," he said.

"What club?" Willow transferred the rest of the hot rolls onto a rack to cool.

"Dane has no family—that's how I became his nursemaid." He put another bite into his mouth. "For me, there was a wife. But she died."

"I'm so sorry to hear that."

"Thanks, it happened years ago. So how did you get to Vermont, then?"

Willow was happy to hear a change in the subject, even to this one. "There was a man. He left. It happens."

"It does." He sipped his coffee.

"So…" Willow had a question that had been bothering her. "The knee. Will it heal properly?" She didn't really want to start a conversation about Dane, but she'd hate to think his career was over, all because of one nasty fall. And, vain as it was, she still felt culpable.

"It will heal," Coach said. "There's no reason to think he won't be training for the Olympics by the fall. It just wasn't that bad a break."

"Well, that's good news," Willow said.

"It is," Coach agreed. "Most definitely."

Twenty

WILLOW PULLED HER truck into the gas station and hopped out with her credit card. She began her transaction only to look up and see that the man filling up his pickup truck in front of her was Travis. She felt her face flush as she locked the nozzle in place. Travis had left her two messages inviting her out to dinner. And she had ignored both of them. She'd been feeling too overwhelmed to be social, especially with someone who might be attracted to her.

"Hi," he said mildly. "How are you doing, Willow?"

"Good, Trav," she smiled, hoping for a neutral topic of conversation to spring forth into her mind. "I'm doing well."

Now *there* was a big fat lie.

"I heard about your injured tenant," Travis chuckled.

"Did you?" Willow asked, hoping to sound impassive. She fiddled with her gloves so she wouldn't have to look him in the eye.

"Sure. The lifties always talk about him. What's it like having a world-renowned asshole living on your property?"

"It's fine, because I never see him," Willow dodged. And it was true.

"At least the rent checks won't bounce." Travis took the nozzle from his truck and hung it back up on the pump.

"Hey, Travis?" Willow asked.

"Yeah?"

"What did you mean that night when you said his family was crazy?"

"Ah," Travis said, folding his arms. "I don't think he's dangerous, exactly." Then his face split into a grin. "In spite of his name, right?" He slapped his leg. "Anyway, his mother was always lurching around town when we were growing up. She was kind of out of it all the time. And then his brother, too. They're just a family of drunks. It turns you into an asshole."

Willow's pump stopped, and she put the nozzle back in its holder. "I'm pretty sure I come from a family of drunks," she said, giving Travis a sideways glance. She capped her fuel tank. It was one of the only things she'd gleaned from her childhood file with the state. She knew almost nothing about her parents, except for the fact that alcoholism had been one of the causes of her removal from their home. "Does that make me an asshole?"

Travis lifted up both hands, like a busted perp. "Willow, come on. I was just running my mouth." His face was red.

Willow knew she was being ridiculous. She had no reason to defend Dane, and Travis had only been good to her. "I'm sorry," she said quickly.

"I'd better get back," Travis sighed. "I'll see you around." He hopped into his truck and started the engine.

She slid behind the steering wheel of the truck, her misery closing in around her.

* * *

Willow and Callie dined together the next day on hospital cafeteria fare. "So, now I have an appointment for an adoption counselor and a baby-care class on the same afternoon. And ten days to decide which appointments to keep."

"I bet that doesn't happen often," Callie said.

"Actually, I bet it does," Willow said. "I can't be the only person who has teetered this long on the fence."

Callie put down her sandwich. "You're right, of course. I didn't mean to be flip."

"It's all right. I know I have to decide soon."

"You're really considering every option, aren't you?"

"Every last one," Willow said.

They were silent a moment, and Callie finished half her sandwich. She brushed the crumbs off her fingers. "Can I ask you a psych question?"

"Sure."

"Suppose there's a prisoner, and he's serving life with no chance for parole." Callie fiddled with the straw in her drink.

"No, you should not get involved with him," Willow laughed.

Callie rolled her eyes. "Very funny. But listen, okay? So, this prisoner has already served a decade, maybe two. Then one day, the warden walks in and says, 'Whoops. We made a big mistake, you're free to go.' My question is this: how does the guy react?"

Willow swallowed a bite of salad. "Well, in the movies, he kisses his lawyer and dances out of prison, to the sound of trumpets and violins," Willow said. "But in real life, probably the opposite would happen."

"What does the opposite look like?" Callie asked.

"People are ruled by their expectations. And if the unexpected happens, even good things, we find it hard to adapt. In real life, the prisoner probably has a total breakdown. He'd punch his lawyer, scream at his mom. Drink himself into a stupor. He might never get over it."

"That's what I was afraid you'd say." The look on her face was far away.

"Callie? Are you letting someone out of prison?"

Her friend looked thoughtful. "Probably not," she said. "But of course, I can't really talk about it." She picked up the other half of her sandwich.

Twenty-one

DANE HAD NEVER felt so trapped and alone.

Coach was always nearby, of course. He went to junior races in Vermont and New Hampshire on the weekend, looking at the up-and-comers. But Dane led an impossibly claustrophobic life in the apartment. Save the occasional follow-up doctor's appointment, there was nowhere to go. He and Coach had tried going out to eat a few times, but it was such a hassle getting in and out of the Jeep, pushing the passenger seat as far back as it would go. And then sitting there in the restaurant feeling like a man with a black cloud hanging over him.

The only thing that brought Dane any pleasure at all was the thing that was causing him so much pain. In the afternoons, after she came home from work, Willow would always visit with her chickens. From one of the two windows in Coach's little living room, he could see an oblique slice of Willow's yard, including the barn door. Dane would stand there waiting, leaning on his crutches until she came out, swinging her egg basket, heading for the door.

If it was a sunny day, the barn would already be open. The chickens always came running like a pack of puppies, swarming Willow's ankles. She always set the basket down and scooped one of them up. The chicken would sit in the crook of her arm while Willow stroked its back. Then she would invariably pull some raisins out of her pocket, and the girls would flap themselves into a frenzy while she doled out these treats, talking to them.

He watched because of the look on her face, which was always peaceful. There was no way to imagine that she wasn't having a really hard time right now. Callie had said as much. But at the same time, at least for the moments when he spied her out the window, she wasn't totally broken. Not yet, anyway.

That made one of them.

* * *

After dark was when Dane had the most trouble. It made the apartment—and his life—feel impossibly small, with nothing to see out the window except for his own ugly reflection looking back at him. On this particular evening— barely distinguishable from all the others—Dane had been channel surfing for half an hour, nothing holding his attention for more than a few minutes.

Coach was beginning to fidget in his chair. "So what's the deal with Willow?" he said.

"What do you mean?" Dane kept his eyes on the screen.

"What do you mean, what do I mean? What's the goddamned problem?" Coached grabbed the remote out of Dane's hand and turned the power off. "I see you watching for her in the backyard. I can only guess why you do that. But when she brings the mail to our door, you won't even glance in her direction. There are twelve-year-old boys with more game than you."

Dane began the difficult chore of getting off the couch. Leaving his legs propped onto the chair, he crab-walked his upper body onto the floor. "I know you're bored, Coach. A few more weeks and we'll be out of here.

You can go find some teenage prodigy to do you proud in case I blow up again before the Olympics." With his hips suspended in the air, Dane pressed up on his fingertips and began a series of dips, working his chest and arms.

Coach looked into his beer bottle. "You're acting like a sorry asshole, Dane. Even for you, this is extreme. I just want to know—what did that nice girl do to you?"

Dane finished a set of thirty before resting his butt on the floor. "You wouldn't be asking if you didn't mean it the other way around. What did I do to *her?*"

Coach leaned on his elbows and looked Dane in the eye. "Fine. What did you do to her?"

"If you want to know so bad, I got her pregnant."

"Fuck." Coach put his head in his hands. "You poor kids."

"Why do you feel sorry for me? She's the one who's knocked up."

The look on Coach's face was the hardest one he'd ever seen there. "Don't *ever* talk to me like I'm stupid, Dane. Just because you don't talk about your problems doesn't mean I don't know what they are."

"You *don't* know what they are."

Coach's stare was unrelenting. "If that's the line you want to take, fine."

"Leave me alone, Coach."

"I leave you alone too much. If you won't talk to me, I think you need to get some help."

Dane snorted. He lifted his hips off the floor again and began another set.

"I have one question, and if you answer it, I won't bring it up again."

Dane lifted his eyes.

"When you look out that window at Willow, what do you see?"

Dane's tightened his abs and decided to press the set to forty reps. "I see someone who punched me in the gut," he ground out.

"That's what love feels like, kid."

Dane adjusted his balance so that he could dip himself with only one arm. Then he reached up and lunged for the remote, snatching it out of Coach's hand. "If you're so wise, what are you doing sitting alone in this shit hole with me?"

Twenty-two

CALLIE WAS DISAPPOINTED to see Willow's truck in the garage when she pulled up the farmhouse driveway. Her friend came smiling to the kitchen door when she opened her car door.

"Callie?" Willow called. "This is a pleasant surprise."

Callie took care to bring both her purse and the calmest face she could muster from the car. "Willow, how come you're not at yoga?"

Willow shrugged. "Didn't feel like it. And you said you couldn't be there."

Callie flinched. "Willow, I need to talk to Dane. But I don't want you to come."

"Why?" she whispered.

"Doctor-patient privilege," Callie whispered.

Willow's mouth fell open. "You're scaring me, Callie."

"Don't be afraid," she said. "No matter what, *you* are going to be fine. Stay here, and put on a kettle for tea?"

"All right," Willow said, her face reluctant.

Callie squeezed her friend's hand, and then forced herself to turn away from Willow's frightened eyes. She continued toward the apartment door, feeling around in her purse for the things she'd brought with her.

* * *

Dane had heard the car pull into Willow's driveway, and then the sound of women's voices. He steeled himself against what was coming. Even so, his palms began to sweat. There were two knocks on the door, and then it opened. Callie appeared on the threshold.

His mouth went dry.

Coach popped up off the couch. "I'll step outside," he said, before Callie could even ask.

"Actually—" the doctor cleared her throat "—I might need you nearby."

"No, you won't," Dane spit out. "Coach, this is private." He wiped his hands on his T-shirt and took a deep breath in through his nose. *Steady*, he coached himself. Whatever the doctor said, it didn't change anything. The die had been cast a long time ago.

Still, he found himself studying Callie's stony face, looking for clues. Doctors gave out test results all the time. Callie probably had plenty of practice delivering bad news. But she couldn't know how desperately he wished he could duck the truth a little longer. Just a few more years of not knowing—that's all he had wanted. And now he couldn't have even that.

Quicker than Dane would have liked, Coach put on his coat and disappeared, shutting the door behind him.

Callie approached the sofa, where Dane sat with his broken leg propped onto a chair. She took something out of her bag and held it up to show him. *A syringe*. "This is a sedative. If you can't control your reaction, if I think you're going to hurt either one of us, I'm going to sedate you."

"You won't need it. My test results won't really be news." In spite of the brave words, his chest felt tight.

With a grim face, Callie drew a piece of paper out of her purse. *Fuck*. He locked a defiant stare onto his face.

"Your test came back, Dane. You're negative for Huntington's. You *don't* have the gene."

A second passed, then two. Dane, his jaw cemented together, was having trouble understanding what she'd said. For a long moment he replayed her words in her head, trying to make sense of them. Then he felt his face sag, and the room got fuzzy around the edges. "No," he heard himself say.

Callie knelt down into his line of sight. "Yes. I have the lab report right here." She handed the paper to him. "You don't have it."

Dane's throat clenched as he took it from her, curling his fist around it, crimping the paper. "It's wrong." It had to be. And whenever the correct diagnosis was eventually revealed, this moment of uncertainty would come back to burn him like a hot poker. He knew how badly misplaced hopes could cut a man. He'd spent his teenaged years waiting for someone to tell him that there'd been a mistake — that Finn would live.

But the disease always won. He'd seen it too many times to believe that he'd be any different.

Callie reached into her purse again and took out a second sheet of paper. "I did two different labs, Dane. Two results, from two different states. Same answer. You're going to have to get old like the rest of us."

"You're a liar," he whispered. It wasn't fair, trying to make him think that.

She shook her head. "I'm not lying."

"Bitch." He stared her down, looking for any sign of weakness. Watching for a flinch.

She returned his gaze with clear eyes. "I did what you asked. Now it's all on you."

When he spoke again, his voice cracked. "You're just fucking with me."

"No, I'm not. And that means every other ugly thought you've ever had, every muscle tremor, those weren't symptoms, okay? You're fine, and now you have to figure out how to live with yourself."

Throwing the beer bottle in his hand was purely a reflex. As he watched, it went whistling past Callie's head, landing with a bright crash on the other side of the room. Along with the sound of shattering glass, he heard a scream of frustration from his own mouth. Then the door flew open and Coach ran inside. "Don't FUCK with me!" Dane yelled.

"Dane!" Coach cried, running across the room. He laid a hand on Dane's shoulder.

But Dane swatted him off, and then swung himself unsteadily to his feet. The room was too hot, and there were too many people in it. He couldn't think. If he could just get outside, the world might become a recognizable place again.

"Sit *down*," Coach ordered.

"I'm leaving," Dane said, his heart galloping around his chest.

Coach tried to press him back toward the couch, but Dane wasn't having it. He swung an arm into his coach's gut, sending the older man stumbling. But because he was standing on just one leg, the swing put Dane off kilter, too. He began to topple.

That's when Callie dove at him, aiming his body back into the sofa. "Hold him!" she yelled, and Coach fumbled towards them both, leaning onto Dane's shoulder, pinning him awkwardly to the couch.

And then he was trapped there, like an animal. His broken knee throbbed, and bile crawled into his throat. The room spun, and he closed his eyes to blot it out.

"Can't believe you made me go there," Callie hissed. He heard a plastic snap, and then felt a hand snatch the back of his sweatpants down. A second later, there was a sharp stab in his ass.

"Oww..." he roared. "Get OFF me." His chest felt as if it would break apart, and the next breath came out as a heated sob.

"You owe me seven-hundred dollars. And you owe Willow an apology," Callie muttered behind him. Her warm hand pressed into his back. Dane wrapped one arm around his face and focused on not throwing up. His limbs began to feel strangely heavy.

* * *

At the sound of shouting, Willow shoved her feet into her shoes and threw open her kitchen door. It was only five quick paces to the apartment door. But when she arrived, it was hard to make sense of what she saw there.

Callie held a syringe in one hand, its plastic top still between her teeth. As Willow watched, she let go of Dane and replaced the cap over the needle.

"What's *happened?*" Willow demanded. Dane lay on the couch, his head buried, his chest heaving.

"Willow, look at me," Callie said. Willow found her friend's comforting face. "It's okay, honey. Everything is *okay*," Callie repeated.

But it couldn't be. Because Coach snatched a piece of paper off the floor as if his life depended on it. After scanning it, he sunk to his knees on the rug and covered his eyes. "My God. I can't believe it."

"Coach," Callie warned. "You're scaring Willow."

Willow strode into the room and took the paper out of Coach's hands. It was a lab report, with a strange name at the top. "Who's Igor Maniac?"

Callie jerked a thumb at Dane, who had melted into the couch. "I made up the name..." Callie's head dropped, as if exhausted. "Willow? The prisoner got let out of jail. I'm not sure what happens next. But right now I need us to go and sit in your kitchen. Put the kettle on, and I'll be there in a minute."

Willow nodded, but her feet wouldn't un-root from the floor.

"Coach?" Callie asked, picking up her purse. He looked up at her, his eyes wet. "Did you know about this?" Callie walked over to Dane, picking up his arm to check his pulse.

Coach nodded. "I dug up his mother's obituary on a hunch."

Callie replaced Dane's arm beside his head. Then she tipped his shoulder against the back of the sofa, so that he wouldn't roll off. "He won't wake up until tomorrow, okay? The next few days will be tough." She handed him her card. "Call me if you think you're in over your head."

"Thank you," he whispered.

* * *

"It's really an amazing disease, in a sick sort of way," Callie told her. "You're absolutely fine for thirty years or so—the symptoms are undetectable until well into adulthood. At first you begin to have muscle spasms, and you become forgetful," Callie said. "And then it just goes downhill from there. Your body fails, and your personality darkens. You can't chew your food or speak. But you don't lose all your marbles until the end, so the patient is always aware of every bit of suffering."

Their cups of tea sat untouched on the table. "Oh, my God," Willow said.

"It's extremely rare. His mother died of it."

"And his brother died," Willow said. "Last month."

"Jeez," Callie said. "He didn't bother to tell me that. No wonder he's batshit crazy. I swear to God, Wills — the guy could not have been a bigger asshole to me if he'd tried."

"So…" Willow put her hands on her belly. "He thought the baby…"

Callie nodded. "Dane never had the test, because he didn't want to know. But then you were pregnant…" She rolled her eyes. "If I didn't have to listen to all his bullshit, it would all sound quite noble. He did it for you, Willow."

"No wonder he was so angry." Willow put her head in her hands. "I was really reckless, Callie. My prescription was lapsed, and I ignored it. I thought I could just skate by."

"Well…" Callie cleared her throat. "Someday he's going to look back on this and realize that you did him a big favor. But it's really hard to say when that day might be. First he's going to have to get past a whole encyclopedia of issues. Survivor's guilt…"

"Anger," Willow added. "Denial, grief, isolation. Even his issues have issues."

Callie smiled. "At least you have the training to understand what he's going through."

"I *knew* there was something, Callie."

"You're a gifted shrink."

"He referred to himself as toxic."

Callie blew out a breath. "He wasn't kidding. He meant it quite literally, didn't he?"

Willow nodded. "And if that's why he was so adamant that I not have the baby…" she rubbed a finger around the rim of her teacup. "That's basically admitting that he wished he'd never been born."

"That's fear talking," Callie said.

"It's years of pain talking. He…he actually *cried.* Right after we…" She cleared her throat. "He sounded broken."

"Don't go all soft on me, Willow. I think you have to leave him out of it, now. And make up your own mind. What does your gut say?"

"My gut is worried about money. How can I even weather a few months with a newborn on nothing? It's not like my temp job will give me a maternity leave."

Callie flinched. "Things could be pretty tight for a while. But with a couple of lucky breaks, you could be a practicing psychologist in a couple years with a great job. It's not impossible."

Willow put her chin on her fist. "If only I knew where to get a lucky break. They are in short supply around here. I do want a child. But is it even fair to have one, if I know I'm on the path to becoming a welfare mom?"

"I'm not going to tell you what to do, Willow," Callie said carefully. "But I do know that being a welfare mom isn't necessarily a permanent condition."

"I just don't know the answer," Willow sighed. "If you have a crystal ball lying around somewhere, don't hold out on me."

"I would never," Callie laughed. "I'd be peering into it myself, trying to figure out if I'm ever going to meet Mr. Right."

Twenty-three

EVEN THOUGH IT was March and the snow had already begun to melt, the temperature outside plunged one more time. Lying on the sofa, Dane listened to the wind howl.

He had spent the last few days in a stupor, barely speaking. After whatever powerful drug Callie had injected wore off, he woke the next day shaking. Coach had been treating him as if he had the flu, bringing him soup and sodas. And at first, he'd felt exactly like a flu patient—he'd had a crushing headache and zero interest in food. He slept for hours at a time.

But as the chill crept in under the door, his shock slowly wore off. This morning, his brain had suddenly come back online. He'd spent the day trying to look at his life through a completely new lens.

And it was excruciating.

Every minute of Dane's past had been colored by dread. Intellectually, he understood that his negative blood test ought to change that. The problem, he was beginning to realize, was that words on a page didn't change *him*. Not overnight, anyway. Instead of joy, he felt scared. He would have fifty more years instead of ten. But since he'd tried so hard to keep people out of his life—except for Finn, who was gone—it was going to be a pretty desolate half-century, unless he underwent a complete personality transplant.

And maybe it was too late. Once an asshole with a death wish, always an asshole with a death wish?

In a matter of days, Dane would get the go-ahead to put weight on his leg and go back out into the world. He would have to start physical therapy. He would have to look people in the eye. He wasn't sure he remembered how.

A heavy cloud of self-loathing hung over him. And whenever he thought of Willow, it twisted his guts into a knot.

Slowly, Dane sat up. When he rose to a standing position, his good knee wobbled. *A tremor,* Dane thought immediately. A beat went by before he remembered the truth. Whatever "tremors" he experienced now were just the sign of a little muscle weakness — the result of lying around like a flu patient. The wobble he'd felt *wasn't* a harbinger of doom. It wasn't the mark of death, or a warning of imminent demise. Any trouble he had with his knees was now the sort of thing that any athlete who took mountains at Porsche-speed might eventually develop.

That idea was quite difficult to swallow. Dane had feared the disease for so long that he didn't know how to stop listening for it.

Picking up one crutch, he hopped over to the window. It was too early in the day to look for Willow. She'd be at work for another hour or two. But when he glanced at the barn, he saw the door bobbling in the wind. As he watched, the latch shook in the breeze, opening and closing a couple of inches with each gust. Her chickens were probably blasted with cold air each time it happened.

That couldn't be good. And Dane had nothing better to do than to go outside and investigate.

While he was putting on his coat, Coach came out of the bedroom to put the tea kettle on. "Where ya goin'?" he asked, puzzled.

"Outside," Dane mumbled. He wasn't ready to discuss all the drama that gone down here this week. The conversation was overdue, and at some point he'd tell Coach how grateful he was for all the care-taking that he had done. But talking about it didn't seem possible yet. He'd spent a decade trying *not* to talk about it. He wouldn't even know where to start.

The older man studied him for a moment, his eyes steady and kind. "Colder than a witch's tit out there. Bundle up."

"Yessir," Dane managed. He hobbled over to his boots in the corner, hopping into the only one that he was allowed to put weight on. He put on gloves and a hat.

Coach had not lied — it was bitter outside. When Dane crutched through the packed-down snow toward the barn, his boot made the kind of squeaky sound against the surface that only occurred during a sub-zero deep freeze.

When he got close enough to see it clearly, it was easy for Dane to diagnose the problem on the barn door. The latch was broken, with the old metal fitting snapped in two. Willow had tried to solve the problem by tying a string between the two pieces and lashing it shut. But the wind was having none of it. Another gust or two, and it was going to snap.

Dane tightened up Willow's temporary fix as best he could. Then he stuck his head back into the apartment and startled Coach. "How do you feel about a trip to the hardware store in town?"

Coach put down the sports section of the newspaper. "It's not like I have a better offer."

* * *

Two hours later, Dane stood inside again, waiting near the window. She was late today. The sun was already setting by the time Willow trotted across the crusty snow, her hand in her pocket where the raisins waited.

As Dane watched, Willow drew up short in front of the barn door. First, she touched the new door latch, testing the slide of the bar through it. Then she turned around.

Dane ducked back into the shadows where she couldn't possibly spot him.

After a moment, Willow turned back to the latch, inspecting it, releasing and fastening it a couple of times. Finally, she opened the door and went inside. Before she could even close the door, Dane glimpsed the fluttering horde leaping at Willow's feet.

It was possibly the smallest favor ever done by a man for the woman carrying his child. But it was something.

Twenty-four

WILLOW WAS NOT at all sure why the fix-it fairies had suddenly descended on her property.

First came the new latch on the barn door. The small gesture touched her, and Willow indulged in the romantic fantasy that someone wanted to take a little care of her. But that was unlikely. The broken latch had probably caused the barn door to bang open and shut all day long, driving Coach and his ornery tenant crazy.

It was probably Coach who set it right. Dane couldn't drive, anyway. So the older man was likely her helper. When she saw him next, she'd planned to thank him.

But the following night, her outside light fixtures mysteriously lit themselves. Both of the old-fashioned sconces framing her kitchen door had been missing their bulbs for an embarrassingly long time. Yet when she drove home from yoga that evening, they burned brightly, welcoming her home.

And — this was a much more complicated fix — the broken section of her garage door had mended itself. For more than a year, the plywood facade of one panel had been steadily splitting, exposing the cheap foam insulation inside. It lent the property a certain trailer park aura that she could really do without. On the other hand, she had no spare money to spend on repairs that weren't strictly necessary.

It took her a day to even notice. But one afternoon, Willow smelled sawdust in her garage. But since she did not shut the old garage door that night, she did not spot the reason.

That night, however, she'd climbed out of bed at eleven o'clock because she heard the scrape and stumble of somebody moving around in the driveway. Tiptoeing to the kitchen window, she watched as someone (standing on one leg) eased the garage door down. Even in the dim light she could see a pale patch where new wood had replaced the old broken part. She heard the sound of faint whistling as a tall, curly-haired figure leaned down to dip a brush into a can of paint.

While Willow watched, he began to paint the new portion of the door.

"Who paints in the dark?" Willow whispered to herself. Nobody normal, that was for sure. But Dane was out there, curly hair poking out of the bottom of his knit cap, just like the first night she'd seen him.

How strange.

She'd spent the last few weeks trying not to think about Dane. But that had become nearly impossible since Callie's big revelation. Dane's life had just been turned on its ear, and she couldn't help wondering what that meant for him.

It's just the psychologist in me that wonders how he's doing, she'd told herself.

Yeah, right.

Staring at the moonlit figure painting her garage door, it was impossible to deny that her interest was more personal.

"I'm not boyfriend material" he'd said that first night, while they waited for the plow truck in his Jeep. Dane wasn't the first man to give a woman that sort of brush-off. But the words sounded different to her now that she knew what he'd been living through. Dane had probably believed that he would never have a partner. That any relationship he began could only end in heartbreak.

Willow's relationships had always ended in heartbreak, even without the help of a fatal disease. Then again, they'd each had the *possibility* of a happy ending. In contrast, Dane must had imagined himself living in a world where everyone else got a fair shot at a happy ending. But not him.

It made her shiver just to imagine it.

There was a sliver of a moon outside, just enough to reflect off the snow. Dane painted the door with slow strokes of the brush. She knew she ought to just go back to bed. But it was too tempting to admire the sturdy set of his shoulders as he moved. And to remember the way his hair had felt between her fingers.

Painting her garage in the dead of night was an odd thing to do. But it was almost fitting. Because every single interaction between them had been unpredictable.

Willow sighed. She really needed more *boring* men in her life. Dane was a bad investment by any measure. She knew this. So why was it so hard to look away? She'd been drawn to him like a moth to the flame, even on that first night. The tug she felt when she looked at him defied all reason. It didn't solve her problems, and it did neither one of them any good.

Even though Willow knew this was true, she kept watching.

After a time, Dane stepped back to admire his work. He took a flashlight out of his pocket and aimed it at the paint job. He touched up the paint in a few places, before finally shutting off the light.

She watched everything, until the job was done and he capped up the paint. She watched until he disappeared back into the apartment.

Willow padded back to her bed and got it. With a hand on her still-flat stomach, she closed her eyes and tried to sleep. But even then, she saw him on the backs of her eyelids. He was smiling at her. He was making espresso in her kitchen. He was passing her a beer in a darkened car.

Stop, Willow commanded herself. He and Coach would disappear at the end of April, when Coach's lease was up. It didn't matter that she wanted to know what he was thinking, or whether he would be able to move on and be happy.

She wasn't really a part of his life, even if she wanted to be.

At least if he moved several thousand miles away, she could stop thinking about him. And maybe stop feeling so crazy.

Twenty-five

"I NEED TO grab the pricing sheet," the guy from the hardware store said into Dane's ear. "Can you hold for a moment?"

"Sure." Dane's voice was scratchy. He had barely spoken to anyone for days.

Some limp elevator music began playing in his ear. Dane looked out the window, where a patch of darkening sky was visible. Supposedly, they were about to get one more winter storm. That would put a damper on his Mr. Fix It plans.

He'd completed several projects already, and had already brainstormed new ones. An old house like Willow's always needed something. At this rate, he could keep his hands busy for a decade. Today's project? Order replacement glass for two small window panes that were visibly cracked.

He also hoped to figure out why Willow's truck engine made a knocking sound every time she started it up. But that was going to be trickier. Because whenever Willow's truck was home, so was Willow.

He didn't want to ask permission, either. Because he didn't want to explain why he did what he did. The truth was that everything he did for Willow was really something he did for himself, too. Since the night when Dr. Callie had brought him unexpected news, he'd had a lot of trouble figuring out how to feel about it. There were times when he caught himself feeling gusts of incredible relief.

Unfortunately, relief was always immediately followed by crushing guilt. Even at this moment, as he listened to an instrumental version of a Pearl Jam tune over the telephone, Dane felt himself standing only a few feet from the precipice of despair. When Finn died seven weeks ago, Dane had only felt numb. But now, thoughts of grief were his constant companions. It wasn't fair that he would live, when Finn and his mother had died.

He was the lucky one, but he'd never behaved as if that were true. How did a lucky person behave, anyway? Was he up to the task?

Dane was saved from answering this giant question by the reappearance of the hardware store guy on the phone.

"Okay," the man said. "You need two panes of glass."

"That's right. They're small, because it's an old divided-light window," he said.

"What are the dimensions?"

"Well, one of them measures ten inches by six," Dane said. "The other one..." he hesitated.

"Do you need to go and measure it?"

Dane chewed on the end of the pen he held in his hand. "The other one looks to be the same size. But it's on the second floor, so I can't be sure."

The hardware man coughed once. "You could, uh, go upstairs and measure it, right?"

"That's the thing, I don't have access to the house," he said.

"Maybe you should just order the one you've already measured," the guy suggested. His voice hinted at impatience. And Dane didn't blame him. Who ordered replacement panes for someone else's windows?

He did. Because fixing little things on Willow's house gave him a way to help her. And at the same time, it gave him something to do with his hands.

Dane gave the hardware store his credit card number and then hung up the phone.

Across the room, Coach stepped into his boots. Dane was grateful that the man hadn't made a single comment about Dane's strange new hobbies. "The storm that's coming could bring us twelve inches of snow. So I'm going for groceries." Coach grabbed his jacket.

"Could you..." He swallowed. "Would you see if Willow has everything she needs?"

Coach tilted his head, his expression soft. "I would do that," he said. "But she isn't home. Callie picked her up a couple of hours ago, they went off to some appointment at the hospital." He snatched his keys off the nail by the door. "I hope they make it back before the snow gets any feistier. See you in an hour." Then he went out the door.

Silence descended on the room, and Dane turned Coach's words over in his mind. *Appointment at the hospital.*

He stood up quickly, bile rising in his throat. Had Willow gone to have an...?

Dane's heart banged against his ribcage. He should already made a proper apology. *Christ.* He should have told her that whatever she decided, it was okay.

He'd been such a shit.

Dane lifted his hands to his head while the room threatened to spin. He could still apologize. He would. But what if she'd already listened? What if she believed he thought she was...all those nasty things he'd said.

He took a deep, shuddering breath.

189

The sound of the wind grew increasingly loud, rattling the roof. Dane got up off the sofa. Pulling his crutches off the floor, he maneuvered over to the window. The snow had begun in earnest about an hour ago, and now Dane saw that the flakes had already covered the patches of grass that had shown through the recent thaw. The window revealed its slice of Willow's yard and the barn beyond. Dane waited, watching.

* * *

Callie dropped Willow off, but couldn't stay. "I have to get home before the roads get worse."

"Thank you for coming with me!" Willow beamed at her friend.

"I wouldn't have missed it," Callie said.

It would be dark in half an hour, and even snowier. So Willow didn't go into the house. Instead, she went into her garage where the feed bags waited. She had already knocked one of the fifty-pound bags onto a kiddie sled. All she had to do was pull it to the barn.

Willow headed out across the yard, the wind whipping her hair all around. When she reached the barn, she opened the door and dragged the chicken feed inside. "Coming through, girls," she said as the sled began to catch on their wood shavings. She scooted forward, toward the feed bin.

This next part would be tricky.

Willow tipped the empty feed bin on its side. Then she tugged the rounded end of the sled into its opening. Moving around behind the sled, she grabbed the back and tried to lever it up, tilting the fifty-pound bag into the bin.

Instead, the plastic sled bent in the middle.

"Damn it," she said. It wasn't going to work. So she squatted over the feed bag and put her hands on either side.

"Can I help you with that?"

Willow whirled around to see Dane leaning in the doorway. There was snow in his hair. He'd grown a beard, which made his face look a bit older and more serious. His expression matched—it was grave and thoughtful. But it was still the same man who made her breath hitch when she looked at him. Those sharp blue eyes and long lashes looked back at her. And then he was moving toward her, the tips of his crutches landing in the wood shavings.

Too surprised to speak, Willow backed out of his way.

Dane laid his crutches on the floor. Then he righted the bin, bent his good knee, picked up the feed bag and dropped it in.

"Thank you," she whispered, feeling rattled. "I've been trying not to lift…" She stopped, clamping her lips together.

He stood up slowly. "*Lift things,*" he said. Then his mouth opened and closed like a fish.

Oh no. She felt herself trembling.

"Willow," he began. Then he put one hand on the wall of the barn to steady himself. "Are you going to have a baby?"

Terrified of his reaction, she only nodded.

Slowly he closed his eyes, lifting one hand to his temple. "God, I'm so relieved."

For a second she couldn't say anything. "You *are?*" she stammered.

He nodded, looking unsteady. "Because…" he said. "Because I didn't *wreck* you, Willow. You made your own

191

call." He tipped his head back with a sigh. "I said awful things, and you stood your ground."

"It wasn't an easy decision, and I don't know if I did the right thing," she said, hearing herself start to babble. "But my gut said I do want a child. The timing is awful, but I really do."

The look on his face was so raw, so vulnerable that it startled her. "You're impressive, Willow. You meet assholes right and left...." He shook his head. "Nobody breaks you. Not the idiot who left you, not me, not the jokers at the bar that night..." he cleared his throat. "Hang on. I didn't even get to say it yet." He bent over and plucked his crutches off the ground. Then he hitched a step closer to her.

She just stared up at him. She had to stop herself from reaching out to touch him, to acknowledge that he was really here, talking to her.

"Willow, I just want to apologize. Everything I said—I wish I could unsay it. I'm just so sorry I was cruel. You deserve so much better."

At that moment, a gust of wind banged the barn door on its hinges, and the chickens stirred in fright.

Willow felt her heart in her throat. "Dane, a blizzard is coming and..." she was suddenly feeling a bit lightheaded. She'd been yearning—no—she'd been *desperate* for his apology. But actually hearing it was scary. The decision to cut him out of her life completely was a painful one, but also uncomplicated. Now here he was, his eyes begging. She didn't know what to do with it.

"There's more I need to say, Willow." His voice was low. "Can we talk in the house?"

She took a deep, steadying breath. "Just...give me a minute." She turned away from him, her heart fluttering.

The chicken feeder was stocked and their water bottle adequately filled. "Hang in there, girls," Willow called. "See you in the morning." She pulled her hood back over her head. She followed Dane out of the barn, sliding the brand new latch back into place.

* * *

Outside, the world was a darkening swirl. Snow coated every surface, and drifts began accumulating at the base of every tree. Willow went ahead of Dane, opening the door to her kitchen. She kicked off her shoes and went to sit on the couch, lighting the table lamp in the corner.

Across the room, Dane struggled to free himself of his one snowy boot. When he eventually came crutching toward her, she watched him approach, half thrilled that he wanted to talk, and half terrified of what he might say.

"Willow," he said, hesitating before her. "You don't have to look at me like that. I'll never say a word against you again."

She took a deep breath and then blew it out. "I think there were extenuating circumstances. Callie told me. What you thought you had…the genetic…"

He maneuvered around the coffee table, then sat down beside her. Slowly, he reached out, covering one of her hands where it lay on the cushion between them. "But I was nasty, Willow. I was mean to the only person…" he bit off the end of the sentence. "I can't get the sound of it out of my head."

She withdrew her hand, then crossed her legs, turning to face him. "I'm sorry, too."

"For what?"

"I wasn't careful, when I said that I was."

He shook his head. "It happens. Usually to people who aren't us."

She studied him, finding his clear eyes steady. She wanted this Dane—the accepting one—to stick around. But she wasn't ready to trust it. "Can I show you something I got today?"

"Anything."

Even then, Willow hesitated. But his blue eyes were patient, waiting. She stood up and pulled the little stack of sonogram pictures out of her pocket, handing them to him. Willow could feel her heart pounding in her ears as he looked at first one and then the others.

"Wow," he whispered, glancing up at her with wonder on his face. "I can't believe this is real."

"That was my reaction, too," she admitted.

He laughed, holding the pictures closer to the lamp. "A tiny little ski-racing chicken farmer." He let the pictures fall into his lap. "I have absolutely no experience with this. So I need to ask, how can I help you?" He cleared his throat. "I need to know. Beyond fixing all the little broken things on the outside of your house. What can I *really* do?"

The question made her heart race. "I…I really have no idea. I never thought you'd ask."

Dane flinched. "That's fair."

"I guess…" She cleared her throat. "I've got it covered for the next six months."

"Okay." He sighed. "Willow, I'm going to be off these crutches soon."

"That's good."

"Sure. But in a couple of weeks, I'm supposed to be headed out west."

Oh.

Willow felt an unnameable pressure in her chest. Whether or not it was a sane reaction, the idea that Dane would go away forever made her unbearably sad. "I see." She looked at her hands.

"Willow?" She looked up to find his handsome jaw set in a serious expression. "If you told me not to go, I wouldn't."

Her heart leapt, but she didn't trust it.

His face was nervous. "I know I don't really deserve it, but I have to ask, because I'll regret it forever if I don't. Is there any way I could spend some time with you?"

Hope began to bubble up inside her, but Willow tried to beat it back. There were still so many issues. "But I'm having a baby you don't want."

He shook his head. "Who *knows* what I want, Willow? For years I never let myself ask. I'm a big mess. But I just...You amaze me, Willow. Every time I see your face, I feel happy."

"I... people don't say those things to me." There was a lump in her throat the size of New England.

"They should. And I wish I'd said it earlier. But I... I quarantined myself. I've *never* had a girlfriend, because I thought it wouldn't be fair to her. That means I've never told anyone I loved her. I've never even said, 'I'll call you tomorrow.' *Christ*..." he broke off, rolling his eyes. "I'm really selling myself here, aren't I?"

Willow couldn't help it. She smiled. "I don't know what to say. I've just spent the last three months trying to get over you. What do you want from me, Dane?"

He put a single finger on the back of her hand, and she felt it like an electric charge. "You know how some people have a bucket list? They want to go bungee jumping in New Zealand, or they want to have sex in an airplane bathroom?"

"Okay…?"

"Well, my bucket list is ass-backwards. I want to fall asleep on your sofa in the middle of a movie. I want to bring you a beer during commercial breaks. I want you to warm up your cold feet with mine."

"I can't drink beer, I'm pregnant."

"Would you *please* come here?" He patted the spot next to him on the sofa.

Her heart skittering, Willow moved over to sit near him, her feet next to his on the coffee table.

Dane slid his arms around her, and she leaned back onto his chest. His body was sturdy and warm. He kissed the top of her head, and she pulled his arms tighter around her midriff. "You have no idea," he whispered, "how happy this makes me. Just this." He gave her a gentle squeeze.

She turned her chin, resting her cheek against his chest.

"The most important thing I want to say to you is this," Dane said, his voice soft. "Every time I walked away from you—since that very first morning—it was always because I thought I needed to. I handled everything very badly, but I only meant to protect us both. It's just that there wasn't any way to do that."

"I'm starting to understand," Willow said.

They were silent a minute, and then he said, "It's hard for me, Willow. Even now, I'm trying not to hear a little voice in my head. The one that says—you'd better get away from that girl, you're toxic." His voice dropped to a whisper. "Don't you dare love her."

Willow's heart beat double-time. "If you want to have a life, you tell that voice to move on now," she whispered.

"I want to," he said, with a halting breath.

Willow raised her head. His eyes were damp. Without thinking, she reached up to stroke his cheek with her thumb. "I've been trying to imagine what it was like for you. To live with the dread of dying young."

"It's not just dying," he said, his voice wrecked. "It's *ugly*, Willow. A nasty wasting away. My father split because he couldn't watch anymore. So I told myself — don't ever be close to anyone. For years I thought I was doing okay, living a big life and keeping everything to myself."

"Until I screwed up your strategy."

His arms tightened around her. "You flattened me, Willow. The day I met you was like doing a face-plant at eighty miles an hour."

"I'm sorry."

"I'm not. I'm wrecked, and I'm rattled. But I'm not sorry." He took a deep breath through his nose.

A silence settled over them both, but it was the good kind. Sitting here with him was easier than she would have imagined. Outside the wind howled and the snow fell into the encroaching darkness, obliterating the footprints they'd made between the barn and the house.

Willow wondered whether the ugly tracks they'd made on each other's hearts could be covered over, too.

"What do you think happens next?" Dane asked in a low voice. "That's a question I never asked myself before. I was always jealous of people who had futures. I didn't ever stop to think that having one would be so complicated."

She stroked his hand where it lay across her stomach. "Just breathe in. Breathe out. Then repeat," she said.

He laughed. "I can try that."

She turned her chin to face him. "So, which movie do you want to fall asleep during first?"

As she watched, a slow smile started on his lips and traveled all the way to his eyes. Then he put his nose in her hair. "I wouldn't even care. You could pick."

"You know," she said, "there's a little voice in my head lately, too."

"What does it say?" His dimple appeared.

"It says," she dropped her voice to a whisper, "popcorn with extra butter." She pushed his hands off her, standing up. She handed him the remote. "You see what's on."

Twenty-six

THEY SETTLED ON an action flick. But Dane could hardly focus on the screen. He was too busy inhaling the strawberry scent of her hair and feeling the warm slant of her back against his chest. When she squeezed his hand during a particularly tense gunfight, he closed his eyes just to concentrate on the sensation of her palm against his. Whenever she shifted against him, his chest expanded with happiness.

The girl felt so good. The nearness of her was like therapy.

"I'm going to be so angry when they kill off that character," she said, pointing at the screen. "The biker dude."

"Hmm?"

"He's going to bite it in the end," she said.

"You've seen this?" he asked.

"No. But that character is a classic overcompensator. He's the sort to take some horrible risk during the final showdown."

He chuckled into her hair. She reached back and swept it over one shoulder, exposing a creamy stretch of her neck. It was right there, under his nose. If he stretched forward a mere inch, he could nibble on it, just a little bit.

No way. Don't wreck it.

The plan for tonight was just to be with her. And it was a good plan. Impulsive sex had caused them plenty of trouble already, and he was willing to wait. So Dane ignored the swelling in his briefs and leaned back on the couch. On screen, the hero crept through a darkened parking garage, a single bullet left in the chamber. From the nearby darkness came the sound of a gun being cocked, and the hero froze.

At this moment of carefully constructed cinematic tension, Willow scooted higher up on Dane's chest, her gorgeous neck even closer to his lips. Dane's dick punched against his pants, and he sent it a silent warning. *Dude, we really aren't going there tonight.*

As soon as the action hero pulled off another daring escape, Willow tipped her head back, then turned her chin, her lips almost touching his ear. Then she exhaled, and her warm breath took him from merely chubby to rock hard.

"Willow," he whispered. "You're making it very hard for a guy to focus on the movie."

She turned his hand over in hers and traced his palm with two of her fingers. "Sorry," she said.

Dane took a deep breath and dialed his arousal down a few notches.

"Hmm," Willow mused. "The sidekick just happens to know how to fly a helicopter? That's convenient." She leaned forward as the copter lifted off the helipad, and Dane decided it might be possible to focus on the screen.

And that's when the power went out, plunging the room into blackness.

Uh oh.

For a moment, neither Dane nor Willow said a word. But the absence of all light and TV noise made it even more obvious to him that his body was pressed up against Willow's in the pitch dark.

Willow groaned. "Now I won't know how it ends."

She turned toward him, so close that he could feel her breath on his chin. He felt such a crackle in the air between him that it might have lit up the room. "I could tell you how it ends," he said.

She reached up and put her hands on his face, which nearly killed him off right there. "Dane, have you seen this movie?"

"I may have."

She was quiet. "Well, spill it already."

"Okay," he said, the heat of her hands seeping into his soul. "The hero drops from the helicopter onto the moving train and shoots the bad guys. Then he rescues his family from the container car."

"Hmm," Willow said, so close that the word vibrated off of the corner of his chin. "That's so predictable. But what about the sidekick?"

By this point, most of the blood in Dane's body had flowed away from his brain and into his shorts. It was hard to think. "The sidekick dies from eating a bad egg-salad sandwich. Not Vermont's finest."

She pinched him.

"Ow," he smiled.

"You haven't seen this movie," she challenged.

"Have so. Coach loves this movie. I just don't want you to feel bad about the ending."

"Tell me," she whispered. "I can take it."

He pressed his forehead to hers. "I forgot who I was dealing with."

"The sidekick bites it, doesn't he?"

Dane let himself nuzzle her face with his nose. It was just the lightest touch—it could barely be said to count against his rule. "Turns out, the terrorist put the bomb in the helicopter, not the train. So the sidekick has to drop the chopper into a ravine, blowing himself up, but saving the city."

"That's depressing," she whispered at close range. "It sounds like something you would do."

"Next time, we'll watch a comedy."

Then Willow kissed him, and the feel of her soft mouth on his was transporting. For a moment he could do nothing but give in and return the kiss. The gentle slide of her tongue between his lips was everything he wanted. *Thank-you, universe.*

But eventually he got a hold of himself, breaking their kiss by turning his chin. "Willow?"

"Yes?" she murmured.

"I've been promising myself I wouldn't do this tonight."

She was quiet for a moment, and he hoped she wouldn't be offended. "Dane," she said quietly. "You make a lot of rules for yourself, don't you?"

"Yeah," he said. "And I never had any trouble following them until the night I ran off the road with you. And now, when we're in the same area code together, I can't keep my head on straight."

"So you made a new rule that you don't want to kiss me tonight."

"Oh, I *want* to kiss you." *And a lot more besides.* "But I told myself I wouldn't, because I need you to trust me. Even if it takes a while."

"Hmm," Willow said, tapping a single finger on his lip. "Then can you do me a favor?"

"Anything."

"Try to find a way to be a little less hot?"

In the darkness, he smoothed her hair down her back and tried not to register the sensation of her breasts pressing against his chest. "I have facial hair and a gimp leg. That should help."

She put her hands on his beard, her fingers tracing a line down his face, toward his neck, which made him want to shout for joy. "That's insufficient," she said.

"It's pitch dark," he argued. "You can't even see me."

She moved away then, and Dane took a deep, steadying breath. The next sound was the strike of a match, and he saw a tiny flame over the coffee table as Willow lit a candle. Then she turned to face him, the yellow light flickering on her skin, shining golden on her hair.

He was in deep, deep trouble.

She curled herself like a cat next to him, her eyes on his. "Two things," she said. And then he almost didn't hear what the two things were, because she took that moment to lick her lips. The appearance of that pink tongue slicking across her perfect mouth made him temporarily deaf. "The first thing," she was saying, "is that apologies are very sexy. Secondly, you made a speech earlier tonight about wanting to do all the ordinary guys do with their girlfriends. What do you suppose they do when the power goes out?"

He slid his hands around her waist and pulled her closer. "I'd give you a witty reply. But I'm finding it hard to think in sentences."

"Dane," she said, and her face wasn't teasing anymore. She looked into his eyes with such wonder that it would have been impossible to look away. "My life could not be more complicated right now. But there's a real connection between us. You can make all the rules you want, and it will still be there." She tipped her head, watching him.

He blew out a breath. "The night I met you, you told me 'instinct is real.' But I've been fighting it my whole life."

"I'm not fearless," Willow said. "I don't want you to break my heart. But hiding from it won't help."

He gazed at her. Willow had surprised him the very first time they'd met. And now he understood that she was the only person he'd ever met who was capable of surprising him every day for the rest of his life. "I want to be more like you," he said. "You face everything head on."

"You did that today," she said. "That's why I can do this." She brought her face close to his, brushing her lips against his.

He closed his eyes then, to the sensation of falling. Clinging to Willow, he heard a moan escape the back of his throat. She silenced it with her lips. Then they were kissing, their mouths wordlessly finishing the conversation. He didn't deserve her, and he told her by sucking gently on her lower lip.

She wanted him anyway, and she expressed this with her fingertips, which caressed his neck, and with her tongue, tasting him and teasing him.

He was so sorry to have hurt her, and his hands cradled her back to tell her so. His fingers slipped beneath the hem of her top, smoothing her soft skin, apologizing. When he opened his eyes, the candlelight danced on the walls, and flickered in the dark pools of her eyes. "Willow," he said, just to hear her name on his own lips. He tipped her carefully onto her side, so that her head rested against his chest, facing him. Then he lifted her top a few inches, placing one hand across her belly. He held it there.

She put her own hand on top of his. "There's nothing to see yet," she whispered.

He stroked her stomach anyway. "Do you feel different?"

Willow nodded. "Morning sickness is real. And some days I'm so tired."

"I'm sorry," he said.

She smiled. "I'm not. It's just temporary."

He dragged a finger across her tummy, just at the waistband of her jeans. She closed her eyes with pleasure, her legs shifting slightly. He felt his own pulse grow ragged with desire. "Willow, is it safe to make love to a pregnant woman?"

Her smile was playful. "If it wasn't, the species would go extinct. Another symptom of pregnancy is that it makes you want to all the time."

"Good to know," he chuckled.

"It has something to do with increased blood flow in the area." She rolled her torso onto his, her breasts pressing against his chest, her face buried in his neck. "Dane?"

"Yeah?"

"Is it safe to make love to a man with a broken leg?"

He stroked her hair. "We could find a way. Maybe not on the kitchen counter."

"I guess the Jeep is out, then?"

* * *

Dane followed Willow and the flickering candle into the bedroom. He eased himself onto her bed, his back against the headboard. "Willow," he said, his voice low.

"Do you have a cushion I could use to prop up the gimp leg?"

"Of course." She found a pillow, and he hauled his knee onto it. She lay down on his other side, her body curled against him. But then she gave a troubled sigh. "This is the scene of the crime," she whispered.

He turned his head sharply. "Don't say that, Willow. I don't regret anything except being mean to you."

"Okay. But I'm still allowed to be a little embarrassed."

He stroked her chin with his thumb. "Really? If our mistake ends up changing my whole outlook on life, will you still be embarrassed?"

Her face was thoughtful. "The trouble is that someday my child will ask me where babies come from. When your mother explained it to you, what did she say? My foster mother said, 'when a man and a woman love each other very much…'"

He kissed her on the head. "I have plenty of time to make an honest woman out of you then," he said. "If you let me, I plan to love you very much."

She didn't say anything, just pressed her face tighter against him.

"Are you okay?"

She gave a little sigh. "Yes. It's just that I can feel the complications pressing in on me."

He put his hands on either side of Willow's ribcage and lifted her, until her beautiful face looked down on his. Then he set her down on his chest, closing his eyes as he found her lips.

Her mouth softened for him, her lips opening to receive him. She caressed his chest with two hands. "It's hard to feel bad when you kiss me," she whispered.

He cupped his hands on her face. "All right. Because I can keep this up a good long time." He was greedy with his next kiss, his lips hungry, his tongue encouraging her. Eventually she began to relax, her body melting onto his, her soft face heavy in his palms.

"Mmm," she said, stretching her leg across his body, straddling his hips. "Is this okay?" she whispered, her eyes flicking back toward his injured leg.

"That is better than okay," he said. He gathered the fabric of her top in his hands, pulling it over her head. It was just incredible to touch her again. He'd spent weeks wanting her, absolutely certain that he would never again have the chance. But here were his fingers, caressing the satin cups of her bra. And here was her hair, sliding over his chest.

"You beautiful thing," he whispered. He reached around her and unclasped the bra. Her breasts bounced free, and he gasped. "Christ," he laughed. "You're huge."

Willow looked down at her breasts, so round and creamy in the candlelight, their nipples taut. "You noticed? It's another side effect of pregnancy. None of my bras fit anymore."

She really had no idea what she did to him. "I *memorized* your body, Willow. Because I was sure I'd never get to touch it again." He cupped her breasts and she winced. He stilled his hand. "That hurts?"

"They're tender."

He lightened his touch, his thumbs just grazing the swollen skin. He pulled her closer, craning his neck. His tongue lightly swept her nipple, which hardened like a pebble where he licked it. Then, supporting her shoulders, he raised her body over his. He opened his lips wide, just resting her breast inside his mouth, holding her aloft to minimize the pressure. Her nipple wet, Willow moaned, her face falling into his hair.

He guided her body back down onto his. He'd worn only athletic pants lately, since they fit over the brace on his knee. The soft pants also accommodated his raging hard-on, which was now right between Willow's legs. As she kissed him, her body rubbed against his. She sighed into his mouth, her hands gripping his back, his neck, roaming into his hair.

He felt like a grenade with the pin pulled.

Dane slipped a hand down the back of the stretchy yoga pants she wore, cupping her bottom. He pushed down the fabric with his other hand, slipping down her pants and her panties together. "Let's get rid of these," he said.

* * *

Willow rolled to the side, avoiding his injured leg. She slipped off the rest of her clothes. "Take off your shirt," she demanded, feeling giddy when he quickly shucked it off. God, he was beautiful. She reached for him, caressing the exquisite muscles on his chest. She could happily traverse the geography of his torso for hours.

Dane scooped one long arm under her knees and swung her across his lap. As one of his big hands traveled down her sternum, Willow got goose bumps. She knew she ought to feel vulnerable right now. Here she was, giving herself to him again. He was a risk, and she was at a frightening juncture in her own life. But his solid body felt like home, and the warmth of his skin soothed her fears.

She twined her fingers in his hair and kissed him again. He sucked on her tongue while his fingers grazed her belly, then slipped between her legs. When he found the deep slick of wetness waiting there, they groaned together. She gasped as he palmed her, spreading the moisture everywhere.

Desire flooding her, Willow clung to his neck, kissing him urgently. Dane slid two fingers inside. As his thumb stroked her swollen bud, she became dizzy with arousal, her hips twitching as he touched her. Her bottom grazed the tip of his cock every time she moved. The heat blooming between her legs was unbearable. "I want you," she murmured.

"You'll have me," he whispered. "Soon."

But he didn't stop. Instead, he thumbed her clit in long, insistent strokes. She was so turned on that every breath brought her closer to the edge. "Oh, Dane," she said. "You'll make me..."

"Come," he said, covering her mouth with his. His fingers plunged inside again, his hand caressing her to even higher heights.

She groaned and felt her body gather into itself, her senses concentrating under his touch. Willow felt the shimmer of orgasm begin, then break across her body like a wave. He kissed her hard as her body contracted, gripping his fingers like an embrace.

His powerful arms tightened around her, and with them came a moment of déjà vu. The very first time he'd touched her had felt just like this—strong but worshipful. From the very beginning, the abundant tenderness of his touch had never wavered. His words had put her through so much misery, but his body had always revealed his true feelings. The truth was there in his first kiss goodbye, and even his grasping hands when he was wracked with fever.

Dane's touch had never lied.

Willow tucked her head against his chin and tried to catch her breath. He rocked her gently in his embrace. "Sweet thing," he whispered. "Holding you makes me so happy."

Her heart fluttered to hear it. The path forward would not be smooth. But if he was determined to find it, then just maybe they would.

Twenty-seven

DANE HELD HER as she came down, her heart rate slowing, her face flushed. His balls throbbed, and for once it was an excellent problem. Because they had all night. And tomorrow. And, if his luck held, many days after that. Her skin against his was a balm for everything that pained him. The quiet contentment that he felt in his chest was a brand new thing.

Eventually Willow began to stir again, her lips brushing his pecs, her eyes flickering into his. He drank it in, sighing as her fingers teased the curly hairs running down his belly. Then she rolled off him, her feet finding the floor next to the bed. Leaning over, she kissed her way from his belly button to the waistband of his athletic pants. His breath hitched when she teased her finger underneath.

She looked up then, a smile on her perfect lips. "Help me do this without hurting you," she said.

Dane pressed his hips off the bed, allowing Willow to draw his pants and boxers down to his thighs. She hovered over him then, her hair draping on his belly, hiding her face. He could only feel it, not see it, as she slowly lowered her tongue to the base of his cock, then licked her way from the base to the tip. "Oh, fuck," he gasped. She flicked her tongue over the tip of him again, and the sensation nearly sent him through the roof.

He was panting when she stood up again, tugging on his trousers. Dane kicked them off of his good leg, and then she moved down the bed, her bare skin golden in the candlelight, and eased the clothing over his broken leg. She bent over to examine his knee, the surgical wound visible through the cutout in the brace. "Ouch," she said, meeting his eyes.

He chuckled, stretching back against the headboard. "I'm not really feeling any pain right now."

"We'll try to keep it that way." She slipped onto the bed, gently straddling him. Her hands grazed his pecs, her thumbs teasing his nipples. She leaned over to kiss his neck, and the line of his beard up his face. She licked and teased and nibbled, and Dane cupped her bottom with eager hands. He wanted her so badly.

She sat back, her face serious. "Can I put pressure right here?" she asked, a hand reaching back to the top of his thigh.

"Try it."

Willow sat back carefully on his hips, her bottom grazing his thighs. Only then did she curve her fingers around his cock. "Is this okay?"

"No problem," he gasped, and she smiled at the strangled sound of his pleasure.

She stroked him very gently, but his eager body wanted so much more. He yearned to wrench his hips up off the bed and roughen her stroke. But it wasn't just his injured knee that held him back. He would savor this. It wasn't just an erotic hour that Willow was offering him, but a chance to have something much more beautiful and lasting. It was a gift, and Dane wanted to appreciate every second.

All at once, Willow rose up, guiding him underneath her body. Her eyes on his, she sank down on him very slowly, inch by tantalizing inch. "Oh, Willow," he gasped. The sensation was so overwhelming that he had to close his eyes. He felt her rise up over him again, then sink exquisitely down once more. The stunning grip of her wet body around his made him pant. Every nerve ending he owned stood at attention. She moved again, this time squeezing his cock from inside her body. "Christ," he said. "You're killing me."

"Kegel exercises," she said. "Pregnant women are supposed to tone up."

He put both of his hands down on her hips, holding her still. "Whew. Hang on a second." Dane flopped his head back against the headboard. He hadn't felt so trigger-happy since he was a teenager. But she didn't obey, instead squeezing him inside her again.

Christ. Christ. Christ. He took another deep breath.

Willow grasped his hands, moving them from her hips to her lower back. "Dane, look at me."

He obeyed, opening his eyes. She arched back into his hands, then rose up, giving him a full view of the place where his wet cock disappeared inside her. She sank down again, her heavy breasts jiggling slightly as she rode him. He sucked in air, trying to hold himself together.

She stilled her body again, leaning forward, her hair dangling in front of her nipples. "Now I need to know something."

He looked up at her, speechless.

"Which is better, this or skiing on fresh powder?"

When his brain cleared enough that he could process the question, he hooted with laughter. Pulling her down on his chest, he told her the truth. "You win, sweet vixen." He kissed her hair, her face. "No contest." Grinning like a fool, he held her tight. They lay there together for a moment, the humor relaxing him.

The wind whipped past Willow's drafty old windows, causing the candle to flicker. He memorized the shadows on the ceiling and vowed never to forget this moment. Willow looped her hands behind his neck again, and Dane had never felt so alive. She smiled down at him, raising her body up on his shaft. Then her eyes fell closed as she sank down on him again, exhaling deeply as she did so.

The laughter had loosened something in his chest, and now the unfamiliar sensation of joy warmed the space around his heart. He was incredibly, unbelievably lucky. He—Dane Hollister—could have this moment and luxuriate in it. There was no need to run away from it, to fear it. He curved his hands around Willow's chest as she moved above him. Her body celebrated him, held him tight, made his senses sing.

Before, sex was just a quick release—a way of stealing a few moments of pleasure before facing the grim truths of his life. Tonight, everything was entirely new. This exquisite moment between the two of them could build a bridge to the next moment. And the one after that.

He'd have to think about that later, though. Because his mind was busy being blown.

Her next deep thrust made both of them groan. He watched her eyes grow glassy, her pink lips parting. She moved a quicker now, grinding against him. "Mmm," she said, her eyes falling closed. "So good." She began to sigh, a look of concentration on her sweet face.

The evidence of her arousal unzipped his control. He let all the feelings come, felt her everywhere on him. "Sweet thing," he warned, flexing beneath her. A delicious tension sunk down his spine.

She gasped, giving another very sturdy grind.

"Willow," he groaned, his body finally beginning to detonate. He pressed his hips up, bucking against her, losing himself. Thrust by tantalizing thrust, he unburdened himself into her body.

Willow's mouth fell open. She was gasping, pressing herself onto him. For her, he thrust one more time, and felt her body grip his, tightening around his cock. A second later she lay moaning into his neck, while he stroked her back with clumsy hands.

He couldn't speak. He only shifted slightly to reassure himself there was no way he could hold her closer. The now familiar tickle behind his eyes began again. As his eyes filled, Dane reached up and wiped them with the back of his hand.

"Are you going to cry every time you touch me?" she whispered, kissing the corner of his eye.

"Is it a deal breaker?" he asked. "You have the strangest effect on me."

She shook her head. "Coming alive has the strangest effect on you. I'll just stock up on tissues."

Dane sank back against the pillow, stroking her hair. He was lucky in every possible way a man could be. It wasn't just the beautiful girl curled at his side—he had a sport he loved, he had money, he had the cool mountain air. Setting aside the broken leg, he even had his health.

The truth was, he'd been lucky for years, but too stupid to appreciate it. And in service to his own self-pity, he'd been difficult to nearly everyone who had the misfortune to wander through his pain.

But now, as he played with a lock of Willow's hair, he felt some of his old anguish lift away. She had given him a second chance—not just with her, but with everything. And he would try not to fuck it up.

* * *

"It's cold in here now," she said, coming back from the bathroom to hop back into bed beside him. "The power outage takes down my furnace."

"Come here," Dane said. "I'll be the one who keeps you warm."

She climbed in next to him, and he gathered her into the crook of his arm. With tentative fingers, he reached for her stomach, stroking the skin. He cupped her belly, his fingers stretching across its width. "So far, everything I know about pregnant ladies I like."

Willow sighed. "But pregnant ladies turn into mommies. With crying babies."

"And what I don't know about *those* could paper Everest. But I won't run from it, Willow."

"Tomorrow," she said sleepily. "We'll talk more tomorrow."

Tomorrow. What a great fucking concept. He stretched out against Willow's body—the way he'd always wanted to—and fell asleep.

* * *

When Dane next opened his eyes, an early-morning light suffused the room. He was in Willow's bed, but something was wrong. Groggy, he tried to sort out what the problem was. His knee was stiff, as it always was in the morning. But there was something else. He heard the TV, which meant the power had come back on in the night. He heard another noise, too.

He sat up fast. "Willow?" He swung his feet off the bed, grabbed his crutches off the floor and hobbled to the bathroom. He found her kneeling over the toilet, trying to hold her hair out of the way while she dry heaved. "Sweet thing," he said, leaning over to capture her hair for her.

She held up a hand. "You don't have to...I've got it."

"I'm not afraid of a little puke," he said, setting his crutches in the corner and handing her a tissue. "Does this happen every morning?"

She nodded, wiping her mouth and throwing the tissue into the toilet. She closed the cover and flushed. When she stood up, he folded her into his chest. "Maybe that's the end of it," she murmured.

"Is there anything that will make you feel better?" he asked.

"It's weird, but food helps. Certain foods, anyway. This is funny—you know what I can't eat anymore?"

"What?" he rubbed her back gently.

"Eggs..." She shuddered. "I can't be in the same building with an omelet. Don't tell The Girls."

"So let's feed you something else. I could make pancakes. It's the only thing I cook."

Willow sighed into his chest. "I don't really have time. If the plow went by, I have to go to work."

"Today?" he asked. He wasn't sure he could let go of her.

She laughed. "Of course. Every dollar counts."

He pushed a strand of hair out of her face. "Can I take you out for dinner tonight? Although you'd have to drive..."

She gave him a squeeze, and he felt it all the way down to his soul. "You and I in a vehicle together? Sounds dangerous. But I like to live on the edge."

* * *

While Willow brushed her teeth, Dane looked around her bedroom for the clothes that had been so hastily discarded. When the phone next to Willow's bed rang, Dane picked it up. "Hello?"

There was a silence on the line for a moment. And then a voice said, "Bloody hell. I can't believe it."

"Good morning, doctor." He sat down on the bed.

Callie grumbled into the phone. "This had better end well."

"Are you going to stab me in the ass again if I don't behave?"

"At least."

"Then I'd better be good," he said. Willow had come to stand over him. She held out her hand for the phone. But he gave her the universal sign for *"just a second."* "I owe you big, Callie. And I don't just mean the bill."

"Oh," Callie groaned. "Don't make me like you *right* away," she said. "It's less fun for me."

Willow took the phone. "Hello?" she said. She made a comically frightened face for Dane's benefit.

"I didn't expect that voice on the phone this morning," Callie said.

"Um, me neither," Willow admitted.

"What is it with you two and snowstorms?"

Willow blushed. "Isn't that what they're for? And then you wake up the next morning and puke a lot. Oh wait—that's just me."

"You won't get any sympathy here, Wills," Callie said. "I spent the blackout at the hospital, listening to the generators hum."

"Sounds like a party."

"Yoga tomorrow? Or are you too...*busy.*"

Willow laughed. "I'll be there."

Twenty-eight

THEY TOOK THE Jeep, for old time's sake, parking on Main Street.

Sitting across from Dane at the town's only Chinese restaurant, Willow felt oddly shy. As he dished rice onto her plate, there was a lull in the conversation. They'd done everything backward, hadn't they? She was almost three months pregnant, and they'd never even dined out together. Willow felt as though that awkward fact had taken a seat at the table beside them.

"Seeing as this is our first date," Dane said, "wasn't I supposed to pull out your chair? Damn, I did it wrong." He took a sip of his Tsingtao beer.

"Dane, we're sitting in a booth."

"I guess I get a pass on that, then." He winked.

Willow helped herself to a dumpling. "So, was Coach ready to send out a search party last night? You went missing for more than twelve hours."

"Are you kidding? Coach was tap dancing around the apartment, happy to be alone. He's had to put up with my sorry ass..." he shook his head. "I've been a miserable jerk."

"You've had quite a lot happen to you."

"I know." He looked sheepish. "Coach wants me to *see someone*." He made his fingers into quotation marks. "But I don't know what a doctor could do for me."

Willow put down her fork. "Well...the doctor's job is to listen—to be that person you can tell all the scary stuff in your head. So you don't try to pour it out on your family, or your coach or..."

"…Your girlfriend," Dane supplied. He took a very deep breath. "Okay, that makes a certain amount of sense."

"The other thing they'd do…" She looked into his very blue eyes. "You've had a traumatic experience. And it lasted years, and that affects your thinking. Remember, in the Jeep, you said, 'Let's compare crappy things that happened today?'"

He nodded.

"Well, you've been playing that game in your head your whole life, right? And you win every round?"

Another nod.

"If you want to join the human race, you have to figure out how to stop winning."

He looked down at his plate.

"The goal is to get to a place where you can hear a friend say, like, 'Oh man, I have a splinter in my left butt cheek.' And you can say, 'Dude, that's terrible!' Only, you'll mean it."

His face cracked into a smile, even though he looked sad.

She threw up her hands. "Sorry. I didn't mean to go all clinical on you. But *that's* what a shrink is supposed to do."

He cleared his throat. "You're really good, aren't you?"

"What do you mean?"

"You're an excellent psychologist."

She shook her head. "I might be, if I ever get the chance."

"I'd really like to see that," Dane said. He helped himself to some General Tso's chicken "So—how would that work? What do you need to do to finish your degree?"

"I've been thinking about it a lot," she said. "I'd need to reconnect with my thesis adviser first. I'd finish the writing, which is actually the easiest part. But then I'd need to do a clinical internship, and there's where it gets tricky. Because I'd need to be in a city with a teaching hospital that takes on grad students in their child psych clinics."

He looked thoughtful. "It doesn't sound impossible."

"It doesn't sound easy."

"What if I could help you?"

She looked up. "How?"

"With money for starters. I never spent my money on anything other than Finn's nursing care."

"He was so lucky to have you," she said softly. "I'm sorry I'll never meet him."

"I'm sorry, too."

"I appreciate your offer to help, but I'm not sure it's practical. It's a pretty deep hole I've got myself in, here. Just to get out of Vermont is going to cost me plenty—to sell the house, to set myself up somewhere I can finish my program. I feel overwhelmed just thinking about it."

"How far underwater are you? If you don't mind my asking."

She caught a piece of broccoli with her chopsticks. "After I pay a realtor's fee, probably thirty or forty thousand dollars. God, it's so embarrassing. At least I don't have any other debt."

"Willow, that's not so bad. The Olympics are eleven months away. It will be my biggest earning year yet."

"Why is that?"

He set down his beer bottle. "You know there's money in this game, right?"

"Do you mean athletes on cereal boxes?" Willow shrugged.

Dane smiled, his whole face lighting up. "I love this about you."

"What?"

"That you aren't part of this circus, that you aren't interested in me just because of all this crap."

"Which crap?"

Dane showed her the label on his jacket. "These guys pay me seventy-thousand dollars a year to wear their stuff."

Willow felt her jaw drop.

"Then there's the money the equipment manufacturers pay, and a commercial here or there for watches or jeans or a sports drink. It adds up fast, at least for the guys who make it onto the podium regularly. The sport still has plenty of ski bums, just trying to pay the freight for hauling ass around the world for races." He squeezed her hand. "I used to be one of those. Before I started winning."

"I'd still like you as a ski bum," she blurted out. Those blue eyes and that curly hair... Even now she found it difficult not to stare.

He took a sip of his beer, his eyes still smiling at her. "I know you would. But the money just sits there in the bank. I don't mean to be depressing, but I thought I was saving up for my own nursing home. And now I get to spend it on you and the baby instead. If I'm really lucky, I'll get to do that in person."

Her heart quivered. The last twenty-four hours with Dane had been great. But there were still so many difficulties.

"Sweet thing, look at me for a second?"

She raised her eyes.

"I know it's supposed to be me who's the poster child for getting one's shit together. But you've had a hard time, too. You're looking at some big changes. And I want you to know that I get that."

Willow felt her eyes mist. "There's a lot to figure out. And I know you have the Olympics coming up. You don't need the distraction."

He reached for her hand. "Three months ago, the Olympics seemed like the most important thing in the world," Dane said. "But really, it's just another handful of races. I know next year is going to be crazy. But it could be a good kind of crazy. You told me, *breathe in, breathe out, repeat*. So that's my strategy. Maybe it should be yours, too."

She toyed with the food on her plate. "But the baby will show up whether I'm ready or not."

"And that's why I want to help. Although, I'm not sure you're ready to make big plans with me. Are you?"

She avoided his eyes with a tiny shake of her head. "I always give my heart away too fast. I just hand it right over. And then I'm shocked when things don't work out. I'm trying hard not to do that again."

Dane rubbed her knuckles with his thumb. "You need some time, and I won't push you. But I wonder if you could take a few days off from work, about two weeks from now?"

"Probably. Why?"

"The U.S. National Championships are coming up— the last big downhill event of the season. It's in California. Let's go watch. You could see what I do."

Willow sat back in her seat, surprised. Could she do that? Dane had an entire life that was foreign to her. But in the midst of trying to figure out her life, flaking off to California wasn't really on the schedule. But when was the last time she had a vacation? Two years ago? Three? "I'd have to get someone to feed The Girls," she mused.

"I think Travis owes you a favor."

She tried not to flinch at the suggestion. "Well...I'd have to ask someone other than Travis."

Dane's eyebrows shot up. "Uh-oh. What happened?"

"We're still friends. But he wanted to be more than friends, and I didn't. I told myself it was because I was pregnant, and he wouldn't want to deal with it. But the truth was, I just didn't see myself with him. And I was still hung up on you." She palmed her forehead. "Even though you weren't speaking to me."

"I'm sorry," he said quickly.

"I know that," she whispered. It was her turn to reach across the table for his hand. "I'll get someone else to help me. I want to go to California."

His face lit up. "Awesome! I'll look at plane tickets tomorrow. And hotels. This will be fun."

The waitress slid their check onto the table, and Willow reached for her purse. But Dane grabbed the slip. "You don't get to pay," he said. "Ever."

She paused, her hand on her wallet. "Why not?"

He sighed. "Because you already did."

They went out into the night together, taking their time strolling back to the car. The snowstorm had brought one last burst of tourists into town for the final week of good skiing that season. She and Dane were just one couple in the stream of happy faces on Main Street.

Dane paused outside Rupert's Bar and Grill. "I guess it wouldn't be cool to go in together for a drink," he said.

Willow peered in through the window. She didn't see Travis behind the bar, but he was almost certainly in there.

So she shook her head. "It's too bad, isn't it? It's the only decent bar in town."

"No biggie," Dane shrugged. "I'd just as soon have one in your kitchen, anyway."

Just then the door flew open, and two of the drunken lifties stumbled onto the sidewalk in front of them. Travis followed, breathing down their necks. "I put up with you chuckleheads for too long," he said. "I see you in here again, and I'm going to call the cops. If Annie presses charges for harassment, I'll be the first guy in line as a witness."

Unfortunately, the third lifty appeared behind Travis just then. His face reddened with drunken rage, he coiled back a fist, which seemed poised to fly into Travis's head.

"Watch…" Willow started to say.

But Dane was faster. Letting one crutch crash to the sidewalk, he brought his elbow down fast and hard on the guy's raised arm.

The action upset the drunk's posture, and he began to topple. Dane hitched himself back, pulling Willow with him before the man fell to the sidewalk.

Travis wheeled around, taking in his prone attacker, and then Dane and Willow.

"Urgh…" the fallen lifty said. He scrambled to his feet. And then after he'd scuttled well out of the way, he shot "asshole," over his shoulder. Then he chased his friends down the street.

"Coward," Dane called after him, chuckling.

But Travis had forgotten about the lifties entirely. Willow felt his glance land on her, and on the protective hand that Dane had wrapped around her midriff when the drunk had flailed past them. Slowly, Travis leaned over and plucked the fallen crutch off the sidewalk, handing it to Dane. "Thanks for the help," he said, his voice low.

"It was nothing," Dane said.

Travis closed his eyes, pinching the bridge of his nose. "I haven't seen either of you in here for a while. Wonder why that is?" He gave Willow a pained smile. "You coming in for a drink, or what?"

Willow swallowed hard, not sure what to say.

Travis held the door open wider. "Come on already," he said. "My treat."

They followed him into the bar. Willow sat down first. And while Dane tried to arrange himself on a bar stool, Travis pulled a pint glass off the rack. "So..." His kind eyes studied her. "What can I put in this glass for you, Wills?"

She met his knowing gaze. "How about cranberry and soda?"

"You got it," he said with a quick nod.

When he walked down the bar, Dane cocked his head toward Travis. "So, when your drink order changes, everybody knows your secret? I never thought about it before."

"Sure, but he already knew. I almost threw up on his shoes a couple of weeks ago. That's when he offered to beat some sense into whoever..." She cleared her throat.

Dane whistled. "I'd be offended if I didn't deserve it."

Travis came back with Willow's drink. He set two packets of crackers down next to it. "That's for your stash," he said with a wink. "Now, what can I get you, dude?" His face was perfectly friendly, but Willow saw his hands grip the bar top as if he might strangle it.

"A St. Pauli Girl would be great, thanks."

"Comin' up."

When he turned away, Dane leaned quickly over to Willow gave her a surreptitious kiss on the cheek. "It's my new favorite beer. Come with me to Germany for a race some time, and we can get you a blouse like the one on the label."

Willow tipped her head back and laughed. "These days, I could almost fill it out. Excuse me, while I visit the ladies' room for the tenth time tonight." It was another fun symptom of pregnancy, having to pee every ten minutes. She squeezed his shoulder on the way toward the door.

* * *

Travis flipped a coaster onto the bar in front of Dane. Then he put the beer bottle down and fixed him with a stare. His expression was just burning up with resentment.

"So just say it already," Dane sighed.

"Okay I will." Travis closed his eyes. "I don't know what went down between you two, but she was *distraught.*" He shook his head. "I don't see how you deserve her."

"I'm not in a position to argue the point right now," Dane said. "But I'm working on it."

"See that you do. Because if you screw this up, I *will* kill you."

Dane nodded. "If I screw this up, I'll let you."

The bartender's smile was sad. "I mean, *goddamn* it. I'm very perceptive, usually," Travis shook his head. "And I didn't have this one figured out."

"Sorry to spoil your record." Dane swigged his beer.

Travis tapped his fingers on the bar, thoughtful. "Look, I should tell you how sorry I was to hear about your brother. Really. I had no idea."

Dane felt the blood rush to his face, and he wondered where Travis had heard about Finn, and what he knew. *Deep breath*, Dane reminded himself. It didn't matter anymore if people knew. The family curse was ending, and he had to get used to the idea. "Thank-you," he stuttered.

"Tough couple of months for you, then." Travis picked up his bar mop and began shining the wooden surface.

"Absolutely," Dane said, taking another swig. "And I handled them piss-poorly." He saw Willow coming back into the bar from the hallway. "But now things are looking up."

"Good answer," Travis smiled. "Guess I won't kill you just yet." He moved down the bar.

Dane watched Willow approach, and it filled him with joy just to see her coming to sit down next to him. He *didn't* deserve her, but she was here anyway.

"Everything okay?" Willow asked, her eyes flicking toward Travis.

He covered her hand with his, amazed at its small size. "He threatened to kill me, but we're cool."

Her eyebrows disappeared into her hair. "How's that?"

He picked her hand up off the bar and kissed it. "It's the kind of thing you can only understand if you have a dick."

Willow smiled at him over the rim of her glass, and it made him want to take her home to bed immediately.

Twenty-nine

THE PA SYSTEM below them announced that the first skier was on course.

"Sweet," Dane said. "So, look uphill. Because it takes longer to brush your teeth than to run a downhill course. This one is under two minutes."

Willow waited. The sky above Lake Tahoe was impossibly blue. She could see it reflected back in Dane's sunglasses. But she wasn't as interested in the view of the lake as in the view of the guy. He was, truth be told, impossibly handsome. His curly hair shone in the sun, and his freshly shaved face smiled down at her.

They'd spent a lot of time together the past two weeks. While Willow was at work, Dane put in grueling days at the gym or physical therapy. In the evenings, he'd taught her all the card games he'd learned from years on the road with other skiers. He was fun and attentive, and surprisingly relaxed, as if a great burden had been lifted from his heart. She gripped his hand and turned her attention uphill.

After a minute, Willow could sense the approach of the skier because shouts of encouragement were audible on the hill above them. Then, as she looked up toward the bend, a figure came shooting into view, crouched into a tuck, legs stretched so far to the side that he ought to have toppled over. Before she could even register the motion, he was centered again, tearing forward at an inhuman speed. A second later, he crossed the finish line—painted red on the snow—to the sound of cheers.

"Jeez!" Willow said. The skier swept around, coming to a stop in front of the crowd. He ripped off his goggles and stared up at the electronic timing board. "That is what you do?" She turned to Dane, her eyes wide.

"Yes, ma'am. Except faster."

"And cockier." She giggled.

"That, too."

Dane rubbed his hands together and pointed up the course. "So, the best seeded racers come down first. The course gets chewed up by the time the guys in the back of the pack come down."

"How is that fair?" Willow asked, staring up the white expanse.

"It isn't really fair," he said. "In most of these races, you get two runs. And then they reverse the order of the seeds on race number two. And there's time trials, for starting fresh…" He laughed. "It's a bunch of technical bullshit, honestly. We put up with it because it's fun to go fast." He scanned the crowd below them. "It's weird being here without skis on."

"Soon," she said, squeezing his hand. "Though, I wouldn't mind seeing you in one of those tight racing suits."

He chuckled. "I'll put one on for you tonight, baby."

The PA system announced that J.P. McCormack was up next.

"Hey—this next guy could win. He's seeded in the middle, but having a great season. If you turn around, we can see his start."

Willow looked toward the video feed on the press box. On the screen, a helmeted, goggled racer poled fast out of the starting gate, then dug into a tuck.

"Come on, J.P.!" Dane clapped. His eyes were glued to the screen. Willow watched Dane's body lean to the right as the skier made his first turn, then lean to the left as the course corrected. It was adorable—as if he were skiing the race with him. The skier made a series of heart stopping turns, hanging his body impossibly low to the surface of the snow.

Next came a jump of such monstrous proportions that Willow held her breath. "Fuck," Dane whispered as the racer's arms windmilled in the air.

The landing was rough, the skier's legs coming down awkwardly, wider apart to her eyes than looked comfortable. He lurched to the right, and Willow heard Dane suck in his breath. But then, miraculously, he corrected his position and tucked again. "Like a boss!" Dane yelled. "Can't believe that worked." His eyes were glued to the screen. "Only two-tenths back on the split!" he said. "He could almost do it."

A minute later, the skier shot into view on the last turn, tucking tight toward the finish. Dane put his fingers to his lips and whistled. The guy glided to a stop about ten feet from them. He absorbed his time with a solemn nod.

Dane cupped a hand to his mouth. "J.P.!"

The guy looked in their direction. When he found Dane's face, his expression went first to surprise. And then he grinned. He kicked his skis off, stacked them together and started over to the fence. "Danger! To what do we owe the honor?"

"That was some sweet recovery, dude. Well played."

Now the guy looked shocked. "Well, thanks. We'll see if I can hold it together for the second run."

Dane clapped him on the back. "Look, in Italy, when I said…"

J.P. waved a hand. "I don't think we're responsible for the things we say right after a bone breaks."

"Well, anyway," Dane cleared his throat. "Nice run."

"Why was he so surprised that you complimented him?" Willow asked after J.P. moved on.

Dane grimaced. "Nothing gets by you, does it?"

"You two don't get along?"

Dane took off his shades and looked at her, his blue eyes especially bright in the wintry glare. "It's not just him. I'm not known for being warm and cuddly."

Willow put her arms around his waist. "I beg to differ."

He grabbed her butt and held her close. "It's true, though," he closed his eyes and gave her one very nice kiss. "Also, I'm not known for showing up with a girlfriend. The men probably think I'm gay."

"Oh, boy," she said, laughing. "Again, I beg to differ." She put her hands inside his jacket. "The men think you're gay. The women's team knows you're not?"

Dane's eyes widened with a deer-in-the-headlights expression. "A couple of them might have figured it out."

"You should see your face right now." They were nose to nose. "You're cute when you're freaking out." She flicked her eyes towards a group of women standing near the press box, all wearing identical United States Ski Team jackets. "They've been staring at us, though. That's the only reason I bring it up."

"Let 'em stare," Dane said. Then he closed his eyes and kissed her again, and it was the sort of kiss that she felt all the way to her toes.

When the next racer took the course, Willow's phone buzzed in her pocket. She had to untangle herself from

Dane's distracted embrace to retrieve it. The text message from Callie read: *You're making out on national television.*

"Geez!" Willow put a hand on her mouth and looked around. Sure enough, there were half a dozen TV cameras aimed all over the finish area. She felt her face get hot.

"What's the matter?" he asked, his eyes on the course.

She put the phone in Dane's hand, but he couldn't make himself look down at it until after the next racer's time was posted. When he read Callie's message, he laughed. "Must be a really slow news day in sports."

* * *

The second round of runs seemed even faster and more nerve wracking than the first. And as if there weren't enough tension in the air, a skier blew up at the top of the course. Willow watched the screen with horror as one young guy seemed to trip, flying toward the fence, skis in the air. Then his body slammed down onto the snow, skis and poles launching away from him in different directions. Willow buried her face in Dane's shoulder.

He clapped an arm around her with a chuckle. "That was total yard sale. But he's getting up. See?"

She peeked at the screen and saw him, head down, collecting his gear.

"He can try again next year," Dane said.

"Ouch," Willow said.

"That's the sport, Willow. Sometimes you're the windshield, sometimes you're the bug." He held her in one arm, eyes glued to the leader board. "J.P. is up next," he said. He leaned forward when his teammate appeared on screen in the start house. The crowd clapped and shouted encouragements, in spite of the fact that the skier couldn't possibly hear them.

Willow held her breath as he poled onto the course, tucking himself into the shape of a human bullet. The first two turns went great, his long legs reaching out like a frog's to grip the snow as he hurtled downhill. "Here comes the jump," Dane said, his hands white knuckled on the fence. "Yeah!" he yelled when J.P. flew gracefully forward and then landed it.

A minute and a half later, it was over and done, J.P. came sailing across the finish line, then whipping around to see his time. He was three-quarters of a second in the lead. "Is that enough?" Willow asked.

"It might be," Dane said, stroking his chin. "He has to sweat it out now."

* * *

In the end, nobody could best him. And Willow watched J.P., his face lit with happiness, step onto the podium to receive a gold medal. As Willow and Dane made their way back across the snow, J.P. clomped by in his ski boots, stopping to clasp Dane on the shoulder. "We're doing *après* in the Cliff Lounge," he said. "You know, after the press conference bullshit. See you up there?"

"Yeah, I think you will," Dane said after a beat. "Thanks, man." When J.P. walked away, he said, "you don't mind, do you? Some beers with the team?"

"Why would I mind?" she asked. "Sounds like the thing to do. Except, I'll be drinking club soda."

"Okay. I'm not that close to these people, so if you're not having fun, we'll leave. They can be pretty rowdy."

"I can handle rowdy," she said. "I suppose we need a sign, though. We don't have one yet."

"A what?"

Willow shook her head. "I keep forgetting that you're from outer space. All couples have a sign—a way of telling the other person that they need to be rescued, or that it's time to leave."

"Huh," Dane said. "Like what?"

"It could be something physical, like squeezing your wrist." Willow grasped his wrist tightly. "Or it could be a word. Something you wouldn't say all the time."

"Like...platypus," Dane suggested.

"That's a little tricky to use in a sentence," Willow said. "We'd better stick with the wrist."

"I need to stretch for a minute," Dane said. "Standing around all day tightened me up." He leaned over, rubbing his knee.

"Ouch," Willow sympathized. The sun was much lower in the sky now, though the feel of its last rays on her face was sublime. "Aw," she pointed. "Look at that." On the bunny slope in front of the lodge, a handful of children were having a lesson. The kids were quite small—maybe three or four years old. It was hard to tell with all the gear on them. "They look like cute little bugs. The helmets make their heads look enormous," she said.

Dane put an arm around her waist, watching quietly. The kids were following the teacher down the hill, making S turns in her tracks, hands on their knees. "That is damned cute," he said finally. He kissed the side of her face. "I never thought about how much fun it would be to teach a little skeeter how to carve turns."

"I know you're still getting used to the idea," she said.

"I'm ignorant, but I'm not unwilling," he said. "I never thought I could have a kid, so I haven't looked at one. Like, ever."

"I know," she said. "Baby steps."

As they moved on, she saw Dane's head still turned to watch the children. "Those are some seriously short skis," he said, holding up his hands about two feet apart. Then he chuckled. "Awesome."

* * *

The Cliff Lounge had beautiful peaked ceilings, exposed beams and a stuffed elk's head on the wall. Willow sat on a leather sofa with Dane. J.P. and a few other guys sprawled on the furniture around them, drinking beer and blowing off steam.

"Let's see the sore knee," Willow said, patting her own lap. She reached down for his ankle and guided the recovering leg up where she could reach it. "Tell me if this is too much," she said.

Dane closed his eyes as she began to work his lower quadriceps. "Christ. You are a superior being, and I am not worthy of your excellence."

"That sore, is it?"

He nodded with a grimace.

"Danger!" called a gruff voice. A giant guy with a red beard appeared over them.

Dane reached up to give him a fist bump. "Folger, that was some sick air you caught on the jump."

Folger had a laugh that was as big as his enormous head. He dropped himself down onto the sofa next to Willow. "I got a little more than I bargained for on that one. Cost me two-tenths of a second that I couldn't afford." He held his hand out to Willow. "I'm Folger. You must be Willow."

"Nice to meet you," she said, breaking off Dane's massage to see her hand disappear into Folger's hairy paw.

"We're all curious as hell about you." Folger shook her hand. "We can't figure out who would put up with Danger for more than a half hour."

Willow looked at her watch. "Well, we've only been here a few minutes. You never know." The whole group guffawed at her answer.

"If you get tired of him, I'm available," Folger offered. "The women are in short supply this evening, since their event is tomorrow."

"Get your own, asshole," Dane said. But his smile was amused.

"Ah, there's the Danger we're used to," J.P. said, kicking his feet onto the coffee table. "I think we're almost ready for another round of beers," he said. "Folger needs a beer. And so does Willow."

She shook her head. "I'll have to pass."

"I hope you don't have a bad case of altitude sickness," he said, signaling the waitress. "If it's your first trip to Tahoe, that can be rough."

"Nah," Dane said. "She's got a bad case of being knocked up."

"Whoa!" The men erupted into cries of amused surprise. "Like a boss!" somebody called out.

But Willow gasped, her face getting hot. "You," she pointed at Dane, "had better find a more polite way of making that announcement."

"Go easy on him," Folger said. "The man is proud of himself. His swimmers made it onto the podium."

"In this crew," J.P. added, "we're not known for being polite. But if you want to teach him a lesson, hide his cane."

"Good idea," she said, reaching across to touch her water glass to J.P.'s beer bottle.

Dane eased his leg to the floor. And then he slipped his arm around her, pulling her closer to him. His lips drew down to her ear. "I'm sorry if I embarrassed you."

She gave him a quick smile. "It's a little too early to tell people."

"You're the authority on that," he said, his voice low. "It's just that I'm starting to get excited about it."

She felt her eyes mist as she met his gaze. The fact that he told the truth was reflected in his face, and in the warm look waiting there for her.

He leaned in, whispering. "When Finn died, I thought there would never be any more family for me. But I was wrong." He kissed her then, and his lips were soft, filling her heart with unexpected joy.

"Great goblins!" Folger cried. "Aliens have stolen Danger and left this guy in his place."

Well before their kiss broke off, Dane's middle finger was raised in Folger's face.

"Okay, maybe it's still him," Folger corrected. "How's the knee, anyway?"

"It's fine." Dane reached for his beer. "You know the drill—lots of tedious therapy. But I'm just so glad to get off crutches."

Folger nodded his oversized head. "Ain't that the truth? All those weeks where you can't drive your own car."

"Wait—do all of you spend time on crutches?" Willow asked.

"Hell, yes," J.P. agreed. "But we're not as bad as the freestyle guys. Watch a mogul competition on TV, and the announcers spend half their time talking about who's had the most recent ligament surgery."

"Crutches are the pits," Folger went on. "You can't carry anything in two hands. I wore a backpack around my own goddamned house. By the end, you're stoked to move around like a normal guy. I couldn't wait to lay my girlfriend down, climb on top of her and fuck her properly. Am I right?"

That earned him a howl of laughter all around.

"Am I right?" Folger asked again, reaching behind Willow to smack Dane on the head. "Though with a baby on the way, you two must be making it happen."

"Dude, I think leisure agrees with Danger," J.P. said, tipping his beer bottle back. "I never saw him smile twice in one day before."

"I was just saving them up," Dane said, adjusting his bad leg.

J.P. shook his head. "You know, I never did get you."

"What's there to get?"

J.P. pointed his beer bottle at Dane. "You have the whole world hanging off the end of your dick, and you never seemed to enjoy it."

"Huh," Dane said, squeezing Willow's hand. "Everybody's a shrink."

She squeezed back.

"You know, if Danger's having a kid, that's great news," Folger said, stroking his goatee. "The entire circuit will be thrilled."

"The circuit doesn't give a rat's ass," Dane said.

"*Au contraire, mon frère,*" Folger said. "If you have a girl and a kid, maybe next year you'll dial that death wish down a notch or two. A man with something to live for should be easier to beat."

Dane snorted. "Have fun trying."

"The preseason smack talk begins already!" J.P. announced.

"Bring it," Dane laughed.

* * *

"I told you those guys were rowdy," Dane said, stripping off his clothes in their hotel room. Willow was already in the bed, her hair spread out on the pillows, looking like an angel. Every night they spent together made him feel luckier than the last.

"They were fun," she said, reaching for him as he slid between the sheets. "I didn't feel the urge to squeeze your wrist or remind you to feed the platypus. That Folger has a mouth on him."

He turned onto his side, his lips against Willow's forehead. "I'll never get sick of this," he said.

"Of what?"

"Climbing into bed at the end of the day, hearing what you have to say."

"Oh. I thought maybe you meant hotel-room sex."

"That's pretty good too," he said, caressing her bare shoulder. Privately, he thought hotel sex was overrated.

Willow's bed was just about the sexiest place he'd ever been.

"This trip is fun," she said, her fingers tracing very distracting circles on his belly. "I like visiting your strange little world."

Dane leaned down, covering her perfect pink lips with his own. The kiss he gave her was deep and slow, the kind you have time for when the girl is for keeps. Then he said, "I'll make you a permanent resident of my strange little world, if you'll let me. I have a couple of ideas."

Willow twisted a lock of his hair around her finger. "Tell me."

"I want you come out west with me this summer." He propped up his head on one hand. "Can you find what you need in Salt Lake City to finish your degree? I could support you, take the pressure off so that you could do your thing. And then, when the time comes, we'll take care of the baby together."

She blew out a breath. "Wow. Really?"

"Really. The timing is a little tricky, but that's life."

"Why?" she asked.

"Well, September fifteenth is your due date. And that's when the downhill training happens in Chile." He began to chuckle. "Coach Harvey is going to love me bailing on that. I can't wait to see his face."

"That sounds like a problem," Willow said, her voice careful.

He shook his head. "No way. They've gotten worse excuses from me." He slipped a hand onto her belly and began to stroke her skin. "I wouldn't miss it, Willow. But if you won't come to Utah with me, that means I'll have to spend the preseason in Vermont with you. And I will, even if they threaten to kick me off the team."

She picked her head up in alarm. "What?"

"Shh," he said, fingertips on her belly. "Don't panic. I'm just asking you to think about coming out west. We'd have to spiff up my condo a little bit. It's got that bachelor look. The bookshelf is a board across a couple of milk crates."

Willow lay still for a moment. "That's big, Dane. But are you sure you're ready to go there? I worry that you never got to ask yourself which girl you'd like to wake up with every morning. I don't want you to think you didn't have a choice."

"Listen," he smiled. "There's only one way to win a downhill race. Right out of the gate, you choose your line. Then you accelerate to eighty or ninety miles an hour, and you don't second-guess yourself. No regrets. I know more about commitment than you think."

He paused to kiss her again and was rewarded with two warm hands gently stroking his chest. "Now, why would I ever want some other girl? Some stranger with an app on her phone to tally up my endorsement deals? You and I have been to the wars together, and now we finally have a chance to be happy." He brushed his lips across hers. "You and Coach are the only two people who know me at all. And I don't find Coach very attractive."

He could see her smiling even in the dim light. "You have thought about this."

"Every day I think about this." Carefully, Dane rolled on top of her, setting his knee gently onto the sheet. "You've taken good care of me. I would like to return the favor," he said. He took a deep breath. "I love you, sweet thing. Say you'll move in with me."

Underneath him, she gave a shaky sigh. "Okay, Dane. I want us to have a real chance."

Dane moved his hips, fitting his erection between her legs. "How shall we celebrate?" he whispered. He kissed her deeply, unable to resist an experimental grind of his hips. His knee seemed to tolerate the position.

"Did Folger inspire you?" Willow breathed.

"He only read my mind. I think about this every day, too."

"Mmm," she said, stroking his ass. "You feel amazing. Just be careful up there."

"I'd risk reinjury," he nipped her neck, "to do it like a boss."

She laughed until he kissed her again. And then there was no more talking—only kisses and sighs. As she wrapped her arms around his back, he hoped she'd never let go again.

The End

Books by Sarina Bowen

The Gravity Series

Coming in From the Cold
Falling From the Sky
Shooting for the Stars

The Ivy Years

The Year We Fell Down
The Year We Hid Away
Blonde Date
The Understatement of the Year
The Shameless Hour

Each month one lucky mailing list participant wins a free
paperback. Sign up for the mailing list at:
http://SarinaBowen.com/contact

|||| ||| || ||||| ||| ||

CPSIA information can be obtained at www.ICGtesting.com
Printed in the USA
BVOW06s2220091215

429908BV00034B/354/P